THE DROWNED PRINCESS

THE OBSIDIAN SPINDLE SAGA
BOOK TEN

RUSSELL NOHELTY

SPECIAL THANKS

Talinda Willard, HyliaKumatora, Chris Roeszler, Amy Teegan, Chip Orlikowski, RHR, Victoria Nohelty, Alexander Joyner, Pierino Gattei, Caspar Williams, Gerald P. McDaniel, Walter Weiss, Sunny Side Up, Kenny Endlich, Amber Reeves, Joshua Bowers, Elias Rosner, Noah Carruba, John "AcesofDeath7" Mullens, Jamie Minnich, Rowan Stone, Taiga Char, BAOCHAU TRAN, Jeff Lewis, Dave Baxter, Chad Bowden, David Irgang, James Kralik, Emerson Kasak, Matthew Johnson, Paul Rose Jr., Shannon, Dr. Charles Elbert Norton III, Edward Nycz Jr., Jessica Meuth, Caledonia, GMarkC, Chris Cheek, Bianca Tatjana Višić Ritorto, John Otway Jr, Brett Bennett, Jason 'XenoPhage' Frisvold, Scott Chisholm, Amanda Sarah, Alexandra Corrsin, Giles Fox, Rick Parker, H, Rob Steinberger, Alec Loases, David Stephenson, Anthony James Frandsen, JohnDoe, Joshua Easter, MadCatter (Cat Fleming), Kevin Potter, Bill Lisse, Michael Szewczyk, Robert Woods Tienken, Ronald L Weston, Karen Haughn, Shem Bingman, Susan Wilson, Brigitte Ziegler, Matt Soucy, Alyssa, Michelle Pelo, Richard A Shirley, PerryC, Elizabeth Kiefer, Tim, Nicolas Mandujano

III, Karen Roads, Rhel ná DecVandé, Zeb Berryman, Al Gonzalez, S. D., Jörn Flath, Rick Radzville, Aaron Loren, Justise Briones(That/Them), Genevieve Slunka, Michael DeCarlo, Kitty Crab, Jeanne L. Warner, Vi Ta, Bridget D Laurent, Jaime Bialer, Wendy Martinez, Nicholas Harezga, Mira Hunter, Cara Reasner, Lori Case, Melevorn, Rebecca Hill, Jane R., Talia Denham, Jordan Harju, Jesse Coe, Greg Levick, and Andrew Messiah.

The Drowned Princess
Book 10 of the Obsidian Spindle Saga

By:
Russell Nohelty

Edited by:
Leah Lederman

Proofread by:
Katrina Roets

Cover by:
JV Arts

Formatting by:
Cat Banks

CHAPTER I

ROSE

I slept like a baby, which was to say I tossed and turned, waking in fits and starts, cranky and desperate to be held. We had been living in Hepit's bar for the better part of two weeks, and while I was happy to have Chelle back, I really wanted our bed, not the lumpy, hard thing that Rama had given us.

I slid out of the covers and set my feet on the cold wooden floor. The sun never shone on the Celestial Realm. iNyanga told me it was because the stars circled it, and not the other way around. The center of the universe had its beauty, sure, but I missed the warmth of a star shining on my face. There wasn't even a moon to brighten the sky, so the whole planet was the type of chilly that bristled the bones, though it stopped short of freezing.

I stepped over to the window that looked out on the anachronistic realm, with huge skyscrapers built next to ancient pagodas and thatched roof homes. The gods had lived through every time period a hundred times over on thousands of worlds, and they brought their favorite eras to their homes and those places they frequented. The bar that acted as both our salvation and our prison would have been perfectly at home in a Shakespearean play, with the banners of earls' houses hanging off the wooden balconies.

We hadn't left the pub since I helped Rama and his friends save Chelle and Nox from the Crystal Keep. Perhaps it was too harsh to call this pub a prison, at least compared to the Keep, but I still felt like the gods trying to endear themselves to us were more jailers than friends.

Chelle wanted to leave and take our chances back on Earth, but I was reluctant. Although we'd managed to save her in the daring escape, we left Gabrielle behind in the Crystal Keep. I didn't trust Rama and the others to rescue her without us, even though they swore to us it was as important to them as saving Nox's soul and reuniting it with the husk of her body that remained.

It was unsettling to run into Nox these days, with that vacant expression of hers. She was, more than any god I had ever known, full of confidence and will. Now, without her soul, she was more like a computer on power-save mode, staring blankly into the middle distance, and returning any question with monotone, uninspired responses.

Still, it was better having her on our side than as a puppet for Zeus and the Board that was hunting us. I didn't buy everything Rama said, but that much I believed. We had humiliated them by absconding with their prizes, and they would stop at nothing to track us down.

Patient as I was, I had grown tired of sitting on my hands. Every day we asked the Circle of Truth—the gods that resisted the Board's influence, which included Rama, Hepit, iNyanga, Aditi, and others who were only spoken about in vague whispers—whether they had finished their plotting. We were always told that it would be a couple more days. I was starting to get the distinct impression they were as lost as we were and so I didn't love the thought of relying on them for our next move.

"Are you okay?" Chelle moaned as she turned over in bed. "Why are you staring out a window at half past gods know when?"

"I think it's morning," I said. "My body says it's morning, at least."

She held out her arms. "Well, my body says it's the middle of the night, so come back to bed."

I wasn't tired, not even a little bit, but I learned over the last few years to cherish every moment with Chelle because I didn't know how many more I would have before we were pulled apart again. She didn't like that kind of talk, but I knew it was only a matter of time.

I crawled back into bed and Chelle wrapped her arms around me. "That's better, isn't it?"

"It's very nice," I said, laying my arm around her shoulder and allowing her to nuzzle into my neck. "I love you."

She adjusted her head, and Albie snuggled on my chest along with his snake brothers and sisters that lived on Chelle's head. I pet each one of them in kind, and it made me miss my dog Cheyenne terribly. I had left her on Earth with Jamil, our wood nymph friend, thinking I would be back soon enough. I suppose I also understood that I might never be back at all. With Chelle in my arms again, I wanted nothing more than for our dog to snuggle up with the rest of the family.

"I love you, too," Chelle said with a yawn. "I know you're antsy about saving Red, but this is the most time we have spent together in, like, ever. No jobs, no school, no walking the dog, even. Am I a bad person that I kind of enjoy it?"

"No," I replied with a small smile. "There are plenty of reasons you're a bad person, but that's not one of them."

"Smart ass." She yawned again. "Your heart is beating really fast right now."

"It always does that when I'm around you," I said, kissing the top of her head.

"Corny," she mumbled. "I love it."

"I love it, too, but I have to admit, I keep waiting for the other shoe to drop."

"Maybe it won't."

"We're on the run from the gods. The other shoe will absolutely drop."

As if on cue, an explosion rocked the building and the floorboards groaned. We launched ourselves off the bed before the wood snapped and our bed crashed into a table on the floor below.

"Well, that could have been worse," I said, looking over the chasm at Chelle.

"I think it's about to," she replied. "The quiet was nice while it lasted."

CHAPTER 2
RED

Turned out jail was just as bad in the Celestial Realm as anywhere else I had been imprisoned. Once the cells were locked down, they paraded me through the cells, bloodied and bruised, as a symbol of what happened when you defied the Board. It didn't have quite the reaction they expected, though, as my every step was met with hollers and cheers that made me smile even though the pain.

After that, I was thrown in solitary confinement, with little more than rotten scraps to eat and stale water to drink. I hadn't seen the outside of the cell since they threw me in. Being confined to a prison cell without anyone to talk to wasn't much of a punishment, as I was used to being on my own for days, months at a time. In some ways, it was a blessing.

Besides, I wasn't really alone. I still had my connection with Rama that we'd used to communicate to each other. I had been beaten within inches of my life, prodded and probed, but none of that severed the connection. For the first few days I stayed frosty, given that his plan had sent me to jail. But it also rescued Chelle and kept Rose safe—

barely—and I was more than happy to trade my freedom for theirs.

"I'm thinking of a number," Rama said.

"Is it seven?" I asked.

He liked playing games with me, at least when he wasn't busy trying to make a plan to save me from my fate. He must have felt sorry for me. I could have done two weeks of solitude standing on my head, but it was nice to have company, even if it was with a god I only half-trusted.

"Higher or lower?"

"Lower," he grumbled.

"So you had literally every other number to deal with, up to and including infinity, and you chose one of the seven numbers that were lower?"

"Six numbers."

"Zero, one, two, three, four, five, six, is seven numbers."

"Zero isn't a number."

"What?" I chuckled. "Then what is it?"

"It's the lack of a number. It's an anti-number."

"What about negative numbers?" I asked. "They're a thing, and zero is right there between one and negative one."

"I don't give much credence to negativity, dear. You should know that by now."

"Is ten a number?" I asked.

"Yes, of course."

"How, when it has zero in it? Or a hundred, or a thousand? Your argument makes no sense."

"Okay," Rama said. "Show me zero of something."

I leaned back on the crystal wall. "I can't show you, because I'm in a cell and you're not."

He sighed. "You're right. I'm sorry. It was just a turn of phrase, a bad one, mind you, but I meant no offense by it."

I slid down to the floor. "How are you coming with my escape plan?"

"Not—not well, I'm afraid."

Rama stammered, something he never did, which showed how dire the situation really was. I had kept myself in high spirits, knowing that if Rama could break Chelle and Nox out of the Crystal Keep, he could do the same for me. That hope had faded with the words he'd just spoken.

"I have faith in you," I said, even though it wasn't true.

"You shouldn't," he replied. "Nox and Chelle were a special case. They were brought to trial before the Board, giving us a window to act. You are under lock and key, with guards watching every minute of every day. Until they move you out of solitary and ease up their watch of you, we are at an impasse."

"Then I have to figure out a way out of this by myself."

"You're not alone, here. We just have to wait for a little while. Just sit tight. We will get you out of there."

I was tired of sitting tight and waiting. Luckily, escaping prisons and making the best of a bad situation were well within my skill set. I wasn't much use in the real world, where people lived in holly-hobby homes and had menial jobs, but in whatever reality I lived in, my special skills had saved my bacon more than I cared to admit.

I groaned. "Is your number three?"

There was no answer. I repeated myself a few times, then called his name. In two weeks of talking with Rama, he had never gone radio silent on me.

"Hello?" I said. "Rama? Is everything all right?"

"Holy—" he said, then I heard an explosion erupt close enough that it stung my ears even miles away. "We're under attack!"

Attack? My first thought turned to Zeus and the Board

having found him, which meant they found Rose and Chelle, too, since he was providing protection to them...and I wasn't there. I was stuck in a stupid cell, helpless.

"Are my friends, all right?" I shouted, getting to my feet and pacing the cell, desperate to get out. "Rama! Answer me!"

It was no use.

I slammed myself against the door, but it was made of solid crystal, which meant my banging did nothing but hurt. I landed with a thud on the floor. *No, no, no, no, no.* I had risked everything for Rose and was willing to give my life for her, but now I was useless, stuck in a cell while my friends were under attack.

For the first time since being brought to solitary, I felt tortured by the silence, and my own ineptitude. I hated it.

CHAPTER 3
ARIEL

"What do you mean the box was empty?" Queen Aine said from her throne in the Emerald Castle. I'd been dreading this conversation since the moment I found the box hidden under the chapel in the first Church of the Six. It was supposed to contain Rapunzel's eye.

"Exactly what I said, ma'am." I breathed in deeply and puffed out my chest. "The box was resting on a pedestal in the center of the room, but it was empty."

I had searched for the left eye of Rapunzel throughout all of Oz and tracked it to the small forest shrine using clues that my mother's spirit had given me. Or perhaps it was not her spirit, but a construction made by Nox to guide me on my way. It had been hard to know which was the truth, but the moment I opened the box, the visions ceased, which told me that I had found the place Nox believed the left eye resided. Except it had been stolen from its resting place.

Queen Aine waved me closer. "Bring the box here. Maybe you are doing it wrong."

I gripped the gilded box tighter. "I know how to open a box."

"Obviously not," she growled at me. "Otherwise, we would have the eye."

I walked up the slick, emerald stairs to her throne and set the box down. Since Queen Aine was a fairy, it was nearly as big as she was, and could have kept her entombed if I simply pushed her inside.

Aine leaned into the box and felt around. "Sometimes there's a secret lever that—"

"I tried that," I said, even though as a queen she could dust me into oblivion in an instant for cutting her off. "It didn't work."

"Well, you have fat fingers. Mine are much smaller and maybe they—crap. There's no secret switch." She slid into the box and leaned her head on the wooden wall. "This is not good."

"I think that's an understatement."

The two Fates, Clotho and Lachesis, said that without the eye, the Dream Realm would fall into chaos. This theft of the eye filled my stomach with a dread so heavy I thought it might drag me to the ground.

"This is no time to despair." Queen Aine fluttered upwards. I didn't know if her words were meant for me or herself, but by the time she rose to my eye level, her face was stern and confident. "I need to see the room."

"It's about two days' ride from here, but I'm sure with your carriages we can make it sooner."

She scoffed. "I don't ride in carriages. Come closer and lean your forehead to me." I did as she asked, and she placed her tiny hands on my scalp. "Good. Now close your eyes and imagine where you found this box. Make it as real as you can in your mind."

I squeezed my eyes shut and remembered the snakes etched into the grooved walls and the cobblestone floor of the old basement. I turned the corner and rebuilt the pedestal where I found the box. After a minute or so, I had a good picture of it in my mind.

"Good, good," she said. "I see it, too."

My feet felt like they fell out from under me, and then I was plunging into a grand abyss. An instant later, I landed again on the ground, my legs shaky enough that I knelt down, stabilizing myself with my hands. We were in the basement of the church.

"There is dark magic here." Queen Aine floated ahead of me through the corridors, toward the pedestal. "I thought I smelled it on the box, but it was faint. Here, its musk is strong. The last time I felt magic this strong was...the Battle for the Heart of Urgu. Epiales's forces reeked of it; Agrona most of all."

"How could she have found this place? Nobody but Nox and myself knew, and it was locked so deep in my brain that I had no idea I even knew about it."

Queen Aine ran her hands along all the walls until she reached a dark gray stone. "Nox is careful, that much is true, but secrets have a way of getting out no matter how guarded you are. They can be unearthed for the right price and with enough time. Or with the right magic."

"So you think Agrona found the eye, then?"

"I don't know, but there was one thing the gods had while they were imprisoned in Urgu, and that's time. I wouldn't put past one of them to have found Nox's secret."

"But...Agrona died in the battle, did she not?"

Queen Aine bowed her head. "Yes. That is why we must talk to the Fates. I have the inklings of a plan, but it is foggy, and I need them to help clarify it."

CHAPTER 4
CHELLE

Well, that was unexpected. Luckily, we were able to roll off the bed before it crashed through the floor, even if we ended up on opposite sides of the gaping hole in our room.

"Are you okay?" I called over to Rose. She had debris and dust in her normally blonde hair from the explosion.

"I'm fine. What just happened?"

The room shook again as if we were being bombed, and I fell to one knee. A beam in the ceiling crashed through the plaster and I rolled out of the way.

"I don't know, but it can't be good." I stepped carefully over to the dresser and grabbed a pair of jeans and a black shirt, while Rose slung a yellow dress over her shoulders. Yes, this was an emergency, but it wasn't our first emergency. We would be damned if people were going to see us in our skivvies. It was one of the many things I learned in the past couple of years: always take time to put on your clothes before rushing into the unknown because you never knew when you would get a chance to change again.

Once I was clothed, I carefully slid around the edges of the room towards Rose. Another explosion rocked the building just as she was taking a big, uneasy step, and so she tilted backward toward the hole. I lunged for her and pulled her toward me to safety.

"Careful there. That's a big hole."

She smiled. "Thanks. I didn't know that. What would I do without you?"

I kissed her, hard and fast, wrapping my arms around the small of her back before another explosion, and then the door slid open.

"Really?" Rama shouted at us. "This place is coming down and you're kissing?"

"You have to take time for the important things," I replied. "And what is as important as love?"

"How about staying alive?" Rama wasn't a frantic person, so it made me nervous to see him so agitated. "Let's go."

I pulled away from Rose and dragged her through the door. I refused to let go of her, no matter what. I had been through enough crazy situations where we'd been separated, and I wasn't interested in going through another one. Bad things happened when she left my side, to both of us. I barely wanted her to brush her teeth without me these days.

"What's happening?" she asked as we careened down the shaky hallway.

The bar below us was covered with broken plaster and dust and had cracked in two when a large section of the wall fell on it. Half the tables had been knocked over or destroyed and strewn about the room. iNyanga and Hepit laid on the ground, unconscious, covered in white plaster dust.

There was another explosion and Rama held us back. A

huge section of the ceiling crashed into the floor, creating a massive crater.

"They found us," Rama said. "We have kept this place a secret for hundreds of years, but somehow, they found us."

"Probably that mouthy door knocker, Patrisiol," Rose said. She was referring to the brass gorgon door knocker that guarded the front door. "She never shuts up."

"Patrisiol has been loyal to us since the beginning. The only new factors in recent memory are you two, and Nox."

"Well, I'm on their most wanted list," I said. "So, I definitely didn't tip them off."

"And I risked my life saving Chelle," Rose added. "I'm not about to send her back to jail, no matter how much I dislike you."

Rama frowned. "You don't like me? I'm hurt."

Rose thought Rama was a cocky showoff who was delaying her from her plan to save Red and get out of the Celestial Realm. I didn't think he was quite so malicious in his intent, though his arrogance certainly rubbed me the wrong way.

"Would you keep moving?" I growled. "This isn't a time for bruised ego. Massage it later."

Rama leapt across the hole in the floor, and we followed. We made it down the stairs just as three figures appeared in the sky through the gaping hole they had blown into the building. I recognized the woman at the front of the group, with her short, blonde hair and a scar down her face.

"Athena."

"Where are they?" the goddess boomed.

Aditi, one of the conspirators, rushed from behind the bar, covered in plaster. She stood before Athena, stoic, her hands clenched in fists of rage. "You're not getting them, Athena. Go away, before you get hurt."

Athena chuckled. "We have discovered your hideout and will raze it to the ground if you don't give us what we want."

Aditi clapped her hands together and a stream of red exploded from them, knocking one of the soldiers with Athena out of the air.

"Come on," Rama said.

"Are you crazy?" Rose replied. "We have to help her."

For an instant, Rama looked past us and to Aditi, then, with a nod, he turned away. "She made her choice. She's willing to give her life to save the cause, and right now, that cause is the two of you and Nox."

"Where is Nox?" I asked as we continued toward the front door, which had been blown from its hinges and scattered into a dozen pieces.

"iNyanga has her."

"In case you haven't noticed," Rose said. "iNyanga is lying unconscious on the barroom floor."

"We don't have time for this. We have to—" Rama grabbed the piece of the door that held Patrisiol and leapt outside. "Oh no."

When I caught up with him, I saw what had him so scared. Ten airships, every bit as imposing as the ship that had captured me, hovered over the alley. A dozen soldiers stood in formation before us, while a few others loaded Nox into one of the ships.

"Not good," Rose said. "Very not good."

"Place me on that door," Patrisiol growled, nodding to a steel door next to us. Rama did so, and then knocked on it. "Come in," she said.

The door swung open, and we dashed through while the soldiers sprinted toward us at full speed.

"That's a handy trick," I said. The walls exploded around us.

"You ain't seen nothing yet," Patrisiol answered with a grin. "Over there."

Rama placed her in a closet and knocked again. This time we leapt inside a brightly lit room, barely missing another explosion.

"Close it!" Rama screamed.

We were standing in a meadow, and a door had been cut into a tree. Rose unlatched my hand from hers and dove to slam the door. The soldiers were only one good lunge from getting through.

"We're safe for a moment," Rama said, panting.

Rose slid down the tree, her eyes wide and wild. "What was that?"

"A fraction of a fraction of a fraction of the strength the Board has at their disposal, and what we can expect from now on. They have turned their sights on us." He stood again and took Patrisiol into his hands. "Can you find us a safe house while we regroup?"

"Absolutely," she replied. "Just give me a minute to orient myself."

"Oh thank goodness." I plopped down on the mossy ground. "I could use a minute to collect myself."

Rose crawled over and curled herself into my arms. "Me too."

At least I still had her, and I wasn't about to let her go. Not if I had anything to say about it. Not even if the whole of the Board's power came down on me.

CHAPTER 5
NIMUE

Everything hurt. Every movement. Every breath. Every gust of wind that came through the windows crashed across my exposed muscles and sinews, searing into me. Hastur, the King in Yellow, had shorn the skin from my body. Nothing mattered anymore except getting relief from the agony that was my existence.

Had it been an hour, a week, a century that I had been imprisoned in Hastur's dungeon under his immense castle? I regretted my life in a way I never had before. I couldn't bear to look at my flayed body. The loss of it had been a boon to the traitorous Cassandra, who was given my skin for pretending to be my guide in my quest to kill the King in Yellow; she betrayed me at the perfect moment.

I reached out to Rapunzel, trying to use magic to connect with her across the chasm of time and space, begging for relief, but she had no answer for me. I failed in my mission to kill Hastur, like so many had before me, and so she had forsaken me. For the first time, I had no plan, and no hope. There was only pain.

The lock to the dungeon opened, and I scrambled to the front of my cell. Every so often, one of the King in Yellow's guards, the princesses who protected him like none other, brought me a loaf of moldy bread and one glass of scalding water. I had never been laid so low to consume such filth, and I refused it the first time, and the second, but by the third I was so ravenous that I chewed the bread and swallowed the water without any qualms.

This time, the princess who came to feed me was the traitor herself, Cassandra, wearing my beautiful, glowing skin, complete with the cracked hole at the center of its chest where a universe of stars swirled and danced. Baba had remade my skin into something terrible to behold; it made me powerful and infinite and beautiful all at once. Seeing it on Cassandra's body made me want to wretch.

"Where is the food?" I asked through gritted teeth.

She knelt down, with none of the regal energy that I brought to my old skin. It hung loose under her arms and chin.

"I have a surprise for you," she whispered.

"No thanks," I said. "Last time you had a surprise, it led me to this."

She reached into her dress and pulled out an oblong black pill. She held it up. "This will nullify the pain for a spell. My gift to you."

Cassandra might have been lying—maybe the pill would kill me—but I didn't care. I welcomed death. I snatched the pill and downed it without water, the corners of it scratching against my shredded throat.

Nothing happened for a long moment, but then there was a whip of wind, one that would cause the worst sort of pain, and it fell against my skin without a twinge. After a minute, my hands stopped shaking, and though I was still a monster, I no longer felt the agony of my condition.

"Why?" I asked. "Why would you do this?"

"It was not me," she said. "Hastur requests an audience with you, and he couldn't rightfully talk to you if you were screaming the whole time, could he?"

"I don't know," I replied, pushing myself to stand. "Perhaps seeing girls laid low is what arouses him."

"Oh, it certainly does, but he has plenty of playthings to satisfy that need." She unlocked the door to the cell. "If you behave, he will offer you a chance to become one of his wards, like me. I suggest you take his offer. Get into his good graces."

"And why would I take advice from you?"

"Because I am still on your side." She slid the door open, but I refused to move. "I have worked for days to give you this opportunity, because I still believe you are our best hope for killing the mad king, but it is your choice. Rest assured, if you don't come with me now, he won't offer again, and then you will be down here until you die, which I promise you will be longer than you care to imagine."

I didn't believe her. That she would come to me in my imprisonment and tell me she was still on my side, and this was all a ploy to get me closer to the King in Yellow so that I could destroy him from within...I didn't believe her.

"How long has it been?" I asked.

"Two weeks, give or take a day. I'm not quite sure how time works on your planet, but Rapunzel once explained to me the workings of time, so that is my best estimate."

"How dare you use her name, after you betrayed her."

"Believe what you will." Cassandra sighed. "Whether I betrayed her, or you, is irrelevant. The King in Yellow extends his invitation to dinner, and if you refuse, I promise that your life will be even less pleasant than it is right now."

"Your promises don't hold much worth with me, but on this I believe you." I took one step out of the cell, followed by another. "Lead the way, princess."

CHAPTER 6

ARIEL

Queen Aine teleported us back to the castle effortlessly. It would have been nice if she could have used that power to help me on my journey to locate the box, so that we might be even closer to solving this mystery, but I held my tongue on the matter. It was impolite to say such things, and I was very sure that the queen would treat impoliteness severely.

She led me once again across the rainbow bridge toward the Obsidian Spindle, which was now home to a permanent tent city of Dreamers waiting to see the Fates. While they were quite polite on our last encounter, now simply passing between them caused grumbling and angry cursing. Several swiped at my leg, and the guards had to break them from us as I stumbled along. The whole operation had taken on a militaristic tone in the past couple of weeks, with dozens of guards called into service to keep the Dreamers in line. Barricades had been erected to hold a path through the angry throngs.

Queen Aine paid them no mind. "Please excuse their unruliness," she said. "It's most displeasing to see them so upset, but tensions are high. These people have only a finite time to return to Earth before their bodies die there and they are stuck here forever. Pressure has been ratcheted up considerably and continues to rise as the truth about their future becomes clearer."

Once we crossed the bridge, the door to the Spindle opened and Lachesis beckoned us forward.

"Great Fate!" one of the Dreamers shouted. "She has blessed us!"

I turned to see the Dreamers rise, screaming to be seen. The force of their movements bowed the barricades and overwhelmed the guards. The crowd stampeded toward the open door.

Queen Aine sighed and clapped her hands together. When she pulled them apart a purple forcefield emanated around her, pushing the Dreamers back. With their retreat, she moved on.

"I have been quite polite to you, as of yet," Queen Aine called out to the crowd. "I have allowed you to invade my castle grounds and even given you amnesty for your transgressions. I assigned my best guards to defend you, and yet, this is how you repay me?"

"I must see the Fates!" one screamed.

"My child is back on Earth!"

"My mother is sick."

"We are working as fast as we can to fix this problem," Queen Aine said. "Trust me when I say it is my top priority. However, until it is addressed, you must remain calm." She closed the force field around a group of unruly Dreamers, and those inside of it shrieked, while the others watched helplessly, gasping in fear. The bubble rose into the air and hovered over the Forgotten Sea. "Or I will drop you all into the sea, and let the mermaids have their way with you. Understood?"

"Please stop," one of the men in the bubble sobbed. "Please."

"DO. YOU. UNDERSTAND?" She annunciated each word. "Or should I drop you to provide a demonstration?"

"We understand!" they each cried, their voices out of sync.

"Louder!"

"We understand!" the group shouted again, this time in chorus.

Queen Aine brought the bubble back over the bridge and dropped the Dreamers to the ground. The guards had been able to retake their positions and regain order.

Queen Aine scanned the mob. "Good. Now, we live in a society, and if you trust me, then trust I am working to fix this problem. And if you do not trust me, then I will see you leave the Land of Oz and take your chances in the wilds of the Dark Domain, or the fog of the Mistreach. Make your own decisions. But if you stay here, you will behave."

The Dreamers murmured, but they were subdued. Satisfied, Queen Aine turned back to the door and walked past Lachesis into the antechamber of the Spindle.

I followed her inside and said, "That was intense."

"People want to be led," Queen Aine answered, matter of fact. "They demand it." She sighed as the door closed. "It is exhausting though, acting as if I have the answers to every question, all day every day."

I didn't believe that for a moment. She relished the stage, the spotlight, having people hang on her every word. However, again I held my tongue because it didn't seem to matter if you loved, respected, or feared her, as long as you bent the knee to her in fealty.

"How do you expect to give Lachesis and Clotho the power to help these people?" I asked. "They don't seem to have much power without the third of them."

Clotho stepped forward. She moved slowly, as if time had taken every bit of speed from her. "By finding the eye of Rapunzel of course."

I reared back. "Are you kidding? I thought I was looking for them because the Dream Realm was in danger of collapsing."

"It is," Lachesis said. The energy was gone from her voice. Her biting tongue was defeated and tired. "Without the ability to send the Dreamers back, there will be chaos. The world, both our realm and the mortal realm, will see a level of death that has not been seen since the Black Plague, and even that will pale in comparison to the destruction that will be wrought if you should fail."

"Please tell us you bring good news," Clotho said.

"To the contrary," Queen Aine said. "I am afraid we have bad news."

I could barely think straight, given what I just learned. I held out the box with my shaky hands, not sure if I was being lied to, manipulated, or simply treated like a child. In any case, I didn't like it, but I opened the box to show them that it was empty.

"This is most troubling." Lachesis's eyes rose to meet mine. "Do you have any idea as to where the missing eye could be?"

"I have one," Queen Aine said. "Ariel, please give Clotho the box." She returned her gaze to Clotho. "Give it a good smell."

I did as I was asked, and Clotho held the box up to her nose. "Dark magic," she whispered.

"The type Agrona used to open the gate to the Nightmare Realm."

"You can't possibly think—" Lachesis said. "I thought a genie opened the portal to the other side."

"Even their powers are finite," Queen Aine said. "What if she used the eye to enhance the genie's powers, and her own, to cut through to the Nightmare Realm?"

Lachesis looked to the ceiling, rolling the idea around for a moment. "It's possible, but the entirety of her castle is gone, and the portal along with it."

"Not to mention that she turned to dust during our last battle."

Queen Aine shook her head. "Nox cleaned everything up after the battle. She wouldn't even let us into the Heart of Urgu for days afterwards. What if she found something that might have helped us and locked it away in her vault?"

"If she found the eye, then why would she send me on a wild goose chase?" I asked.

Queen Aine shrugged. "Seems simple to me. She didn't think there would be a great battle, that she would find the eye, or that she would be taken from us. Your memories were embedded in your mind centuries ago, before any of this happened."

"So everything I've done is worthless?" I asked. "That's...depressing."

Lachesis frowned. "No, it's not worthless. It put us on the path, and if what Queen Aine said is true, then you still have an important part to play."

It all connected in my brain. "You want me to return to the sea and search through Nox's keep."

"Nobody knows it better than you," Clotho said, holding her hands out. "Will you do this for us, for the whole of Urgu?"

"I will," I replied solemnly. I dreaded seeing my family again. Even though I had only been away a short time, everything had changed since I'd last seen Ursula.

CHAPTER 7

CHELLE

"Rest here for a minute," Rama said. We stopped in the forest under the shade of a large redwood. We'd been walking through the woods for a dozen hours or more, and while he was still spry, my legs were killing me. "I know you humans are weak and frail."

"We're not weak," Rose replied, sitting on a hollowed-out log. "We're mortal. It's different."

Technically, I wasn't a mortal. I wasn't quite immortal, either. I wasn't sure I was even supposed to exist, given that Nox created me from pure magic without the permission of the Board. However, when I looked into Rose's eyes, I could tell she wouldn't take kindly to me calling her out on a technicality, so I simply let her fume.

"How is it different?" he asked. "No matter how you are weak, that does not change the fact that you're weak."

"You gods could have made us stronger," Rose snapped back. "That's on you."

"She's got you there," Patrisiol said from under Rama's arm.

"Come on, Patrisiol." Rama laughed. "You know better. Don't encourage them."

"Wait, what does she know?" Rose asked. "And seriously, does every word out of your mouth have to be condescending?"

"Seems that way," Rama said with a grin and a nod. "Do you really think we gods all had an equal hand in creating you? Some of my kin went and did that behind my back. But it's not like we had a vote one day and said, 'do we want to make humans, yes or no?'"

"Then how did it happen?"

"That is a long and complicated process that started as an experiment and grew over time. Zeus and Odin convinced us that it was a good idea, and then, poof, you were everywhere. I'll admit, the universe has been much more interesting with you around. The animals and plants that inhabited the universe before you were boring."

"I'm glad we can entertain you," I said with a yawn.

"Yes, it's nice, but you are entertaining in the most horrible ways. Wars, famines, murder, and all of these simply terrible things we didn't know the universe was capable of before you came along."

"So, what? There were no wars before we came around? Cuz I'm pretty sure I read about a lot of battles between gods in my day," Rose said. "A lot, a lot."

"Well, war between immortals is kind of stupid, especially since we can't die by any natural means. We have fought each other before, but it has never been anything quite so widespread as total war like you humans engage in way too often. Did you know that on some planets in the galaxy they have warred themselves—their whole planet— to death?"

"Doesn't sound much worse than what we're doing on

Earth," I said. "The world is heating up to a point that it's literally uninhabitable, and half the planet is convinced it's a hoax. Every year it gets worse and worse, and meanwhile we're squabbling about the dumbest things."

"Ha!" Rama said. "Excuse me for laughing, but that's exactly the kind of short-sightedness that comes with mortality. You think only of your own puny lives and can't grasp the enormity of eternity."

"If we're so laughable," Rose said, "then why are you even letting us hang around? Why even try to help us?"

"Because you are the fly in the ointment, aren't you? The entire universe was humming along quite nicely until you infected every corner of it, and in doing so, you created a lot of bad, just oh so much bad, but you are also completely unpredictable, which makes you the perfect catalyst for change."

"Just because we are so short-sighted?"

"Precisely. Gods, me included, look at every angle, and understand that we will have to exist in this universe for the whole of time. But you, by the gods, you will just run into a burning building to save a cat or run into a prison to save a loved one, as the case may be, even if it means you will die." He knelt down next to us. "Your impulsiveness and spontaneity are the exact reasons why we can't contain you, and why we need your help."

"And we are willing to help you," Rose said. "We live in this universe too, after all, but can you, like, stop insulting us all the time? It's not endearing, and it makes me want to slap you."

"Here, here," I replied with a light chuckle. "I can't believe you got Rose to say that she wants to slap you. She's the most patient human being on the planet."

Rama pursed his lips. "You're right. My apologies. I

haven't dealt with humanity in a long time; not since I was one of you, at least, and I forget what it's like to be bound to a mortal coil."

"Wait, you were one of us?" I sat up. "And you hate us? How can you rue our creation when it literally means you wouldn't exist?"

"You think existence is a blessing? Oh, you poor, sweet girl."

"Just stop being a dick," I said, tired of his bluster. "That's not too much to ask. We'll help you fix whatever is broken, but just don't make us regret it."

Rose placed her hand in mine. "Exactly. Now, can you please tell me why we're wandering around the woods, and whether or not we're lost?"

"We're not lost," Patrisoil said. "I know the door is close but—" She sniffed the air. "There it is. Go right."

Rama trudged toward a big tree at the far end of the clearing, and out of earshot of us. When he was gone, I laid my head on Rose's shoulder. "Maybe we can just go. How hard can it be to survive in the woods?"

"Gwen didn't seem to like it much," Rose replied. "And I don't like bugs when they get into the apartment. Imagine how I would do when they were literally crawling on everything? I've already nearly had three panic attacks just thinking about it."

"You have the blessing of two gods," I said. "And I am some type of being made from pure magic. I think we can survive some bugs...or blow them out of the air if nothing else."

"You're right." Rose shuddered. "They are just so creepy."

"Then we'll find somewhere without bugs, and without

gods. I mean, I know they are powerful, but there has to be somewhere in the universe where they won't look for us."

Rose sighed. "I think it's easier to just try to save the universe."

"Doesn't sound easier to me."

Rose was quiet, and then after a long moment, her eyes narrowed. "Fine, you're right. It's probably not easier, but I...I like being a hero, Chelle. I like making a difference. If what Rama and the others said about the Board influencing the direction of the world by deciding who gets to be in charge...if that's true, we can literally change every planet, including ours. We can change the direction of our own destruction by helping Rama and the Circle of Truth. We may be able to find a place where the gods won't look for us, but it will still be ruled by terrible people, and those are the types of people who will be rewarded." She shook her head. "I don't want to live like that. If there's a chance we can make it better, I want to try." She squeezed my hand. "You don't have to, though. You can go."

I pulled her closer to me. "I don't know that I want to go, honestly. The gods betrayed me before, and I'm sick of fixing their mistakes. I don't know if I have it in me to help them again."

"I understand that," Rose said. "It's not my favorite thing to do, either, but it's the right thing to do."

"And if it leads to our deaths?"

"Then we'll meet up in Hell, outside of Persephone's palace, in Dis, just like we planned."

I rose up and kissed her gently. "God, you really always look at the bright side, don't you?"

She shrugged. "It's the only way I can keep going."

CHAPTER 8
RED

"Rama!" I shouted, my voice hoarse. Hours of shouting led to nothing but silence. *Was he dead?* It wasn't impossible to kill a god. I had killed Epiales in the Underworld with my golden dagger, and if I could kill a god, then any god, even Rama, could die.

I fell back onto the hard crystal slab they had welded to the corner of the solitary cell. Who knew how many other prisoners had laid on it or how much bodily fluid was caked into the sheets? I tried not to think about it, but then my mind shot back to worrying about what happened to Rose, Chelle, and Rama. There was an attack, that much was easy to discern, but had anyone survived? Was the Board bringing prisoners back to the Crystal Keep? Would I see them in the cell block if they ever let me out of solitary, or would they be brought to judgement immediately? Would I be able to say goodbye to my friends before the end?

While my brain toggled between these options, I heard an unfamiliar sound. The lock to the door, which hadn't been opened since I was thrown into this horrible room, clicked, and the door creaked open.

"Get up," a familiar voice growled. I couldn't see Athena, save for a blurry outline against the bright lights, but I'd recognize her voice anywhere. She had tortured me within inches of my life the last time we met, with a contented smile on her face. She was a sadist.

No, a sadist would have to acknowledge me as a being with feelings and get off on my screams. She was more of a psychopath. She didn't seem to know or care that I could feel pain. She went about her business like it was any other job, as if she were a filing clerk at the DMV, or a fry cook at McDonald's.

When I didn't immediately hop to my feet, Athena lunged into the room and yanked me up by the collar, tearing the thin fabric of my jumpsuit.

"March," she growled, shoving me down the hallway. "I don't have time for your insolence today."

I hadn't seen the light in days. Even though I wasn't quite human, my eyes clearly hadn't gotten the message, because everything was a white blur. I listened, though, to doors opening and closing, the murmurs of the cell block. I made out blotchy outlines of other creatures in yellow jumpsuits.

Athena didn't let me drift too close to any of the cells, zapping me with a lightning rod whenever I stumbled too close out of the preordained path she had assigned me, one which she failed to tell me about but quickly figured out led straight down the middle of the cell block.

"Where are you taking me?" I asked. "Am I going back to the general population?"

"You wish." Athena hit me again with her rod, sending electricity coursing through my body. I screamed out in pain and dropped to the ground, heaving. She kicked me. "Get up."

She pulled me to my feet with one hand, and my blurry vision came into focus on the jagged scar that crossed her face. I would have pitied her losing her once-beautiful face if she hadn't been such a miserable god.

I faced forward and she jabbed me in the back, at least without the electricity on this time. My legs wobbled under me. I hadn't used them much since entering solitary, and they felt like they had fallen asleep under the terrible force of the lightning rod.

The mutters and murmurs coalesced into a cheer as more of the prisoners recognized me, and by the time we reached the other end of the block, they were yelling uproariously. The outburst brought a smile to my face, but only deepened the scowl on Athena's. I thought she would give me another shock, but that only seemed to rile up the prisoners, so she simply pushed me through the doors at the end of the cell block.

"Don't smile," Athena said, seething at the grin off my face. "They aren't cheering for you."

"Sounds like they were," I replied.

She directed me down a set of stairs that led into a darkened hallway "They would cheer for a dishtowel if it gave them false hope. You have done them more harm than good, in truth. We have quadrupled the guards and reduced rations for the whole prison. Now, we will decrease them further, until they learn you are not a martyr or a hero."

"You can't prevent people from hoping."

She scoffed. "That's what you think. Do you think you were the first person to lead a prison riot and try to escape?"

"Honestly, yes I do," I said.

"So prideful." Athena knocked me in the knees, and the sudden shock of her baton caused me to cry out in pain.

"You are just one more dissident, and I've made my career making people like you crumble."

I steadied myself. "Sounds like you've had a terrible career."

"I've kept the peace."

"Through brute force and fear."

"Any way I needed to." She pushed me forward. "Everyone wants peace, but they are unwilling or unable to understand what must be done to maintain it. I have no such qualms."

"Any peace based on fear is no peace at all."

"Spoken like a naïve child," she growled. "Don't speak again, or these blasts I've given you will start to hurt."

Start to hurt? They were already excruciating. Athena turned up the knob on her baton and it crackled with the increased power. I wanted to be stronger, to defy her and speak again, but I couldn't bring myself to do anything but put one foot in front of the other.

We exited the prison tunnels and headed up some stairs into a room with several marble statues pointing toward the center of the room, and a horrible depiction of humanity suffering under the thumb of the gods etched on the ground.

A massive set of doors stood before us, but we didn't enter them. Instead, Athena pulled me to the other end of the circular room and through a pair of mahogany doors, stained red and carved with dragons on one side and a giant wolf on the other.

The hallway beyond the doors was lined with red-stained wooden doors that appeared sporadically, each carved more intricately than the last. We passed gilded depictions of the gods on either wall until we reached the end, where stood the most elaborate of the doors, engraved with lightning bolts destroying a town of humans.

She knocked, and the door slid open.

"Ah, Athena," a voice boomed. "Have you brought our guest?"

"Yes, Lord Zeus."

She shoved me into the room, which was a combination of the new and the old. A wooden, oak desk took up half the far wall, surrounded by marble tile that continued down a set of stairs and led into a darkened hallway. Bubbling beakers and blinking servers covered the crystal walls. The man in the center of the room wore a lab coat and worked futzing with something on a table.

He turned to me. His chest was broad, and his face wrinkled but still youthful somehow, with a long, white beard touching his exposed naval.

"Good, I want her to see this," Zeus said with a gruff, stern voice.

He made a couple of button strokes into a console, so that the table shifted and turned upright, revealing an unconscious woman I knew very well.

Nox.

CHAPTER 9
NIMUE

I followed Cassandra up the stairs of the dungeon into the main hall of the castle. I had only been in this room once before, when it was filled with hundreds of revelers and partygoers. Without the benefit of all those people to fill the space, Cassandra's heels echoed against the walls, and I realized how much bigger it was than I remembered.

"The King in Yellow is very excited to dine with you," Cassandra said.

"I'd like to talk about the fact that you betrayed me."

"In time, you will see the truth." She turned to me. "I am one of the few beings in this universe that know how you are feeling, having been stripped of my own skin." She pressed the loose skin under her eye back into place. "I could be a great ally."

"It's only because of you that I'm like this," I hissed.

"We are both victims," Cassandra said. "I was hoping you would realize that. Yes, perhaps my actions paint me in a harsh light, but let us both remember who the real enemy is."

I took a step forward. "You are all my enemies. Hastur,

the princesses, you, Rapunzel for denying me, and Baba for forcing me into a deal I was ill-equipped to handle."

Before turning me into a beautiful horror, Baba forced me to agree to kill the King in Yellow or be her prisoner for all eternity. Now, I realized that the reason Cassandra didn't make the deal herself was that she knew the duplicitous nature of her allegiances, and that I would be cursed by Baba for all my days should I ever make it out from under Hastur's thumb.

Cassandra shrugged. "If all you got out of your time here was that nobody can be trusted, then I believe that is a lesson worth having."

"I have learned that lesson over and over again in my life." A tear fell down my face and I couldn't control another from coming, though they stung. "The last thing I needed to be taught was that nobody can be trusted."

Cassandra continued walking. "And yet, you kept trusting people. You trusted Hera with your power, then the Unseelie Court, and then dark magic to save you, and then Rapunzel, and finally me. Perhaps it is a lesson you must keep learning because you continue to fall into the trap of its false comfort. It is your failing."

Her words silenced me. It was an astute observation. She glossed over several other people I had trusted in my journey, like Etsop, and Gwen, and Queen Aine. They were uneasy allegiances, but I trusted them all the same. All the while they were fomenting insurrection against me.

Of course, that was the problem of ruling, and why somebody like Cassandra could never do it. You could not carry out every command on your own, and even the most cautious ruler needed to endow others with the responsibility of carrying out their orders. Even Hastur, powerful as he was, trusted Cassandra to fetch me from the dungeon, and all this time with me she openly articulated her desire to bring him down.

"Perhaps you are right, Cassandra." Appeasement was easy compared to explaining a nuanced position to somebody, especially a nobody I had no interest in speaking to because she was a traitor and also because she was a dullard. "I will take that under consideration."

"Do so," Cassandra said. "Because the last person you should trust is Hastur. He will feed off of it and twist it against you until you lose yourself in his charms." She turned back to me one more time, skin hanging from her chin. "And believe me, for all his faults, Hastur is as charming as he is cruel, and will make you feel like the center of the world before he drops you into a pit of despair."

"Yes, he is a man. I've met them before. I am very aware of how they operate."

CHAPTER 10

ROSE

"Over here!" Rama shouted.

Chelle and I sat on the hollow tree trunk, enjoying the quiet of the forest. In that minute I forgot about the fact that the Board was after us, and that it was our duty to bring down the most powerful gods in the universe.

"That was nice," Chelle said as she kissed me one more time. "Once more into the breach, I guess."

"You have to enjoy the little moments. They're all we've got."

Chelle squeezed my hand. "I never knew how true that was until recently."

We stood together and walked over to Rama, who had placed Patrisiol on a door carved into a giant tree. When Rama knocked, the door opened into a white light. I knew the minute we stepped through, everything would change yet again, and I grew heavy at the thought of it.

"Come on," Rama said.

"What's on the other side?" I asked.

"It's a safe house where we can regroup."

Chelle pulled me closer. "We are perfectly happy to

regroup here."

"We're out in the open here. There's no cover. If Zeus finds out that we're here, we're sitting ducks."

"What's your plan?" I asked. "And I'm not talking about your plan to get us to safety, but I know enough gods to know you're scheming something. You had two weeks to come up with something, and before I take one more step, I need you to tell me your plan."

"It's not so much a plan as a series of ideas tha—"

"Just tell us!" Chelle barked, stiffening her back. "Why does everything have to be a chore with you gods? For once, tell us straight."

I pressed my hand on her back. "I think Chelle's angry because we've been pawns in the gods' games before, and this whole situation gives me that same familiar feeling. Am I wrong?"

Rama shook his head. "You're not pawns. That makes this all seem like a game, and it's not a game. The future of the universe is at stake, and we have this one moment to act."

Chelle rolled her eyes. "Heard that before."

"Lived that before," I added. "We're not new to this game you gods are playing, and before you say anything, yes, I do think it's a game, a game you play with human lives for your own amusement since we can die, and you cannot."

"It's…more complicated than that."

"Not to us."

He held up his hand. "Fine, you're right. If you are going to do your part in this grand plan, then you need to know the truth. The truth is that there is a very good reason why we use humans as the…pawns, to use your word, even though I don't like it."

"Don't care, really," Chelle growled again. "This isn't a semantics argument. It's our lives."

"For once, talk to us plainly."

"It's because the gods cannot take action against each other. The Board sees to that, and by the state of our bond to each other, we cannot kill each other, but humanity..."

"Humans can kill gods," I said.

He nodded. "And they can interfere with our plans, which is why even though you are mortal, the gods fear humanity. You're like a...well, what is a poisonous spider or something on your planet?"

"Black widow," Chelle said.

"Yes, and I would assume that while you could squash a black widow underfoot, given the right circumstances, it could be the end of you."

"I'm not sure if a black widow could kill a human, but a brown recluse could," Chelle mused. I looked at Chelle. "What? I know about spiders, okay?"

"I just didn't know that about you," I replied. "It's nice we can still surprise each other, even after all this time."

Chelle kissed me. "That's very sweet, but I think we have bigger things to discuss now."

"Right." My eyes narrowed and I refocused on Rama. "That is the first explanation I have heard that actually makes sense. So how do we kill a god?"

He chuckled. "Of course your mind goes there. This is what I need you for, because even though it's possible, there are precious few weapons that can. One of them is my staff, the Brahmastra, which is tipped with an incredibly rare substance that can kill a god, at least when wielded by a human."

"So you need us to find this Brahmastra." Chelle said pointedly.

"Partially. I believe we have narrowed our search to a planet, but our search has been in vain despite all our searching."

"We can go," I said. "Chelle is great at finding things."

He winced. "That is where things get complicated. I need Chelle to come with me...to meet an old friend."

"Who?" Chelle asked.

"Odin, one of the most powerful gods, who was kicked off the Board some years ago for subverting their rules. He has a powerful contingent of friends, and with him on our side, we stand a real chance of taking down the Board."

"And why me?" Chelle asked, crossing her arms.

"Because you were a part of Nox's plan and every god knows it, including Odin. She created you for a reason, and many of us believe that reason will lead to our salvation. With you on our side, we finally have a good shot of winning. If we can convince Odin of that, then we stand a shot of making real change in the universe."

"Fine," I said. "Then we'll meet with Odin and then go find the weapon. This really isn't that hard."

Rama hesitated. "It's not that easy. Finding Odin will be difficult, and every minute we don't have the Brahmastra delays our path to victory."

Chelle's eyes flashed. "You want us to split up."

"No, I need you to split up."

"If we have to—" I started, but Chelle stepped forward.

"No, I'm not doing that. I don't care if the universe implodes tomorrow. I'm not leaving Rose again. No way, no how. Find another way."

Rama held out his hands in a helpless gesture. "There is no other way."

"It looks like the universe is screwed, then."

CHAPTER 11
RED

"Good eye, my dear," Zeus said with a smile. He wrapped a collar around Nox's neck. There was no recognition in her eyes, just a cold stare, like a robot that had been powered down. "This is your dear Nox, or what is left of her."

"What are you doing to her?" I shouted. I tried to take a step forward, but Athena pulled me by my hair and threw me to the ground, cracking the back of my head onto the hard marble and sending a stinging pain into my forehead.

"Stay down!" she growled.

I propped myself up on my elbows, wincing, and watched Zeus work. "Let her go."

"Oh, no, my dear. I don't think I'm going to do that." Zeus opened a compartment on a server and pulled out a collection of wires. Rose had forced me to watch enough medical dramas that I recognized them as electrodes, and he spent some moments placing pads at the end of them before attaching them onto her head and chest. "I need her to prove my theory."

"What are you doing to her?" I asked, the pain in my head sapping the fight from my voice.

"I was hasty the last time we met," he said. "I pulled the soul from Nox prematurely. You see, she has information I need, and unless I reattach her soul to her body, it is impossible for me to retrieve it, great and powerful as I am."

"So, you're reattaching her soul to her body? Even Rama can do that, and he's nowhere near the most powerful god I've ever met."

Athena cracked me across the side of the head, and the intensity of my headache grew. "Watch your tone!"

"It's okay, Athena," Zeus said, without looking up. "Stay your hand. I can take care of her, though as always, I appreciate your dogged loyalty to our cause." He fiddled with some dials. "Yes, the process for attaching a soul back to a body is something even a simpleton god like Rama can achieve, but if I simply returned her soul to her body, she would be the same cantankerous sod who opposed me for so long. I believe I have found a way to tweak the process to make the recipient more malleable, while leaving their memories undamaged."

"You want to make her a slave to your will, then?" I asked, flinching at the possibility of Athena's fist, but it never came.

"Why, yes. Yes, I do. I know many of your kind find the idea of slavery gauche, but great empires were built on the backs of slaves. Great things are rarely accomplished without exerting force on an unwilling population. I can see that is not an opinion you share, and why would you? You have never led anything in your whole, miserable life."

"No, I have spent my life fighting against oppression."

"Yes, but you have never *led*. You have never had to exert your will to make greatness, to create from nothing." He knelt to my level. "We should have never given you humans free will, in retrospect. That was our greatest failure."

I gathered what remained of my strength and lunged forward, wringing Zeus's neck with all the strength I could muster. However, even at my full power, all he did was smile and laugh at my antics until Athena pulled me off him.

"There is quite a bit of fire in your belly. I can see why you have been such a thorn in our side for so long." He rose to his feet and rubbed his neck. "That almost hurt."

"I'll kill you if you touch her, Zeus," I growled. "I promise you that."

"Better than you have tried, and each one has failed."

I swung my arms at him. "Epiales said something similar, before I shoved a dagger into his chest and laid him dead on the ground." It was a lie, and it pinched my stomach to talk ill of the dead. Epiales had committed great atrocities, but he died well, as a sacrifice to help save the Underworld.

A smile ticked onto Zeus's face. "Yes, I heard about that. Humans are fascinating. You can snap their neck in an instant, and they barely live long enough for you to pay them notice, but then, they can do something so surprising even you cannot fathom it." He turned back to his machine. "It really is the most fascinating thing about you."

Athena jerked me closer to her. "This one claims to have killed one of us, and you knew? Why was she not punished?"

Zeus shrugged. "Epiales was a thorn in our side, and his death, while a tragedy, removed one more failure point from the equation of the universe. He was always a problem child, just like his mother." He adjusted an electrode on Nox's neck. " Let us see if we can't fix that, shall we?"

He finished placing the electrodes and pulled a glowing blue cube from one of his desk drawers. I recognized it as the same cube that he'd used to trap Nox's soul.

"Is that her?" I asked.

He opened a window on his console and slid the cube inside. "Yes. You might call it her consciousness, or her soul. Everything that makes up Nox is contained in this little cube."

"You've come a long way from sentencing gods to the Dream Realm."

Zeus had used the Dream Realm as his personal prison for gods whom he felt were too troublesome to exist in the universe, but he was not alone. Odin, Brahma, Osiris, and others sentenced their biggest problems to live in Urgu with Hypnos and Nox as their jailers.

Zeus chuckled. "Yes, that was crude, but we have improved the process since then. It's far more humane now."

"There is nothing humane about keeping souls prisoner," I replied.

He shook his head. "It is just like a naïve human to say something like that. There is so much you do not understand about the cosmos. More than you could understand in your entire measly lifetime."

"I understand enough to know what you're doing is wrong."

"Things are never quite so white and black as that, my dear." He finished typing into his console and then turned to me. "Now, let us begin."

CHAPTER 12

ROSE

I dropped my hand from Chelle's. "What do you mean you won't help?"

The hurt in her eyes was palpable. "Exactly what I said. I'm not going to risk my life for them if I have to be separated from you again."

"You don't mean that."

"I told you I didn't know what I would do, and now I've made my choice. I'm not helping them if it means losing you for even one second."

She reached for my shoulder, but I took a step backward, lowering my eyes. "I know that it's a pain to keep being dragged into this, but I can't turn my back on the universe like that."

"We don't owe them anything." Anger bubbled in Chelle's voice. "I can't believe you're not with me on this—after everything we've been through." She took a deep breath, and softness returned to her voice. "I can't believe you are willing to risk our lives for this creep."

Rama frowned. "Too mean."

"Not mean enough," Chelle shot back.

My heart broke as her resolve sunk in. Chelle was a lot of things, but selfish wasn't one of them, and all I could think with everything that came out of her mouth was how bitter and selfish she was being. I didn't much like being dragged into the gods' business, either, but I couldn't turn my back when the fate of Earth was at stake.

"I don't think you know what you're saying," I said softly.

She scowled at me. "You sound brainwashed, Rose. Frankly, you sound like a sucker."

My arms shook and my hands curled into tight balls, ready to strike. I blew the anger out of my nose, trying to calm myself, but the fury rose in my belly. "You want me to run away with you and hide, but I am not a coward. I didn't think you were one, either."

"Ladies," Rama said, his palms outward, but we both glared at him with enough venom that he dropped his hands and stepped back. "Never mind."

"I'm not a coward," Chelle said. "I'm just tired of being the whipping child of the gods. I saved the Dream Realm. I literally died, and all I got for my troubles was a trip to Hell. No special treatment, no thank you, just a life of servitude."

"And I saved you from that."

"You did, and we saved the Underworld together. For that, I was given the chance to return to the Dream Realm as a servant, as one of the Fates, destined to work at the behest of the gods forever." She choked back tears. "Then, when you saved me from that life and Nox brought me back to Earth, I thought maybe, maybe then we could be happy. But you were forced into service defending magical beings, and I went along, dutifully, because I loved you. Now, I find out that my freedom wasn't freedom at all, but just a part in the gods' games, and I was nothing but a pawn in it, yet again." She cut her arm across her body. "Enough, I'm done with it."

I bit the side of my cheek. "And don't you think I'm done with it, too? I saved three realms, and here I am again, pulled into another conflict, forced to save you—"

"I never asked you to save me!" Chelle screamed.

"I couldn't let you die!" I threw my hands in the air, tears streaming down my face. "I couldn't let you rot in prison. I will never let you..." But my voice trailed away before I could finish those words.

"You can, though. You can let me go, because that's what you're saying to me right now. If I don't become a slave to the gods' whims yet again, then you're going alone, isn't that right?"

I swallowed loudly, and then let out a shuddering breath. "I'm saying I can't let the universe suffer for my self-ishness. I want those things you want. I want a quiet life. I want to be with you..."

"No, you don't, Rose," Chelle sighed. "You never did. You used to be jealous that I had an exciting life, and when you became Queen of Oz, it was like a light filled you that never turned on when you were with me. You keep falling into these roles because gods like this guy"—she jabbed a thumb over her shoulder at Rama—"gods like this stroke your ego, and after being a nothing for your whole life, you are so desperate to be important that you will fall for their bullshit, just because they say you're valuable." She stopped, panting, and wiped her nose. "You were always valuable to me, though. I just wish I was enough for you."

I took her hands. "You are worth everything to me, Chelle. I'm sorry if you don't believe that, but it's true."

"Then I will ask you again to come away with me.

Forget this whole thing. We don't need it. We only need each other."

She squeezed my hands and pulled me closer. Her fingers fit into my hands perfectly.

"If I go with you, I will never be able to look myself in the eyes again. I will grow to hate myself, and hate you for it. So, no, I can't." I unwrapped my hands from hers and stepped toward the white door where Rama stood.

I watched Chelle's heart break. I never thought it would happen, but this was bigger than us. Maybe she was right. Maybe I desperately wanted to be needed by everyone, but we were both small parts in this big universe, and if I can be of value to it, I had to try to help.

Chelle looked at me, then at Rama, and then the woods. Then she did it again. And then she said, "And I am with you, so let's go."

"You don't have to—"

She held up her hand. "That's the difference between you and me. You are desperate to be of value to the whole universe, and I just want to be of value to you."

"But—"

She put up her finger. "Don't. Let's just go."

With that, the three of us disappeared into the ether, and my heart broke in a way it never had before. I knew I could never repair what had just been shattered between Chelle and me.

CHAPTER 13
ARIEL

The darkness of the sea used to give me comfort, but now it signaled my oppression at the hand of my adopted mother. No, she was not a mother to me, adopted or otherwise. A mother had some care for their wards, even if it was tenuous. Ursula was simply my jailer.

I could not let my bitterness towards her cloud my path forward. I needed to get to Nox's keep, hidden deep below the mermaids that guarded Ursula's kingdom. My chest tightened as the light from Urgu faded. It took a long time for my eyes to adjust to the oppressive abyss.

The army of the mermaids lurked all around me. I heard their ranks parting as I passed, and my shoulders clamped backward in terror at the brood undulating on either side of me.

"Lux," I muttered, creating a bit of light to guide me. I eschewed any of the means that could have brought me to the bottom of the sea more quickly, as they were all controlled by my moth—Ursula, and would have surely brought me in conflict with her.

Descending by my own devices, I could hope to avoid

her. It would not be so hard now, as Nox's cavern laid a ways from the castle, near the furthest edges of the sea before it began to curl back up and touch the land again. The way was arduous, but I had cast a spell to allow me to cut through the water faster. It was a desperately lonely affair all the same.

"You're faster than last time I saw you, Ariel." I heard a muffled, familiar voice in the deep and my back prickled. I turned to see an orange mermaid, full of flash and pomp. Only the royal family was given the gift of color, and Vivian's was more vibrant than all the others, giving her the divine right to rule once Ursula had given up the throne, or been overthrown.

She was my sister, but only in the way any in the Dream Realm were sisters, or family at all. It was rare for multiple members of the same family to end up in Urgu, and if they did, it was often generations apart. The process for passing through the Veil was complex and relied as much on luck as anything. Vivian had come to Urgu a hundred years after me, and she had a confidence that I would never possess, even if given a thousand more years.

"Sister," I said.

"Mother will be so pleased you returned," she said. "She did not believe you would come back after slighting her as you did, but I never had a doubt. You always were a sentimental fool for this place."

"How did you find me?"

"It helps to have friends among the army, and good hearing." She pointed behind her, where I saw the outline of a mermaid dart forward. "Thank you, Phineas. You have served me well."

The mermaid kissed Vivian's hand. "Thank you, mistress."

"Now, return to your post before you are missed."

Phineas nodded and took off toward the surface again, to be with the rest of the army patrolling far above us. I watched him disappear then turned back to Vivian, who looked at me with a devious grin.

"I don't want any trouble," I said.

"Then you shouldn't have returned," she said. "Ursula is furious at you for defying her and ordered me to return you to her by any means necessary should you make an appearance in our kingdom again."

"Why did the army let me pass through?" I asked.

"To trap you in here, of course. If you tried to return to the surface, you would find it quite the fruitless endeavor."

I never had the command of magic that she did, but now that Hypnos had given me his blessing, I was formidable with magic. It was the only thing that gave me the confidence to return to the water in the first place.

"Just let me go, Vivian. Tell Urs—Mother—that she was right, and you couldn't find me."

"So that you can go around and cause trouble? How would that make me look? I don't think so." She grabbed my arm. "Now, come with me peacefully. You are in no position to resist."

"That's what you think."

CHAPTER 14

CHELLE

I never thought our stances on whether to help the gods would be the thing that broke us apart. Obviously, the gods could force us apart and they had done it before, but I never thought Rose would side with them over us. I never felt so betrayed in my life. I knew that she was a goodie-two shoes who always wanted everyone to like her, but I didn't think she would risk her own life helping the same people who so blatantly oppressed us.

"Here we are," Rama said when we came through the white light and entered the foyer of an elaborate mansion straight out of regency romance. "Home sweet home."

On the walls were elaborate tapestries of Rama winning all manner of battles, mixed with elaborate paintings lined with luxurious frames. The floors were black obsidian and narrow red carpets led down the long hallway toward a spiraling staircase. He funneled us through the foyer and down the hallway, following the plush red carpet along the way.

"Welcome home, sir," a dark-skinned woman said with

a bow. She wore a yellow and red sari. "Would you like tea?"

"Please," he said. "And two cups for our guests. Is their room ready?"

She nodded. "I turned it down myself this morning."

"Marvelous." He bent and kissed her hand. "You are a wonder."

We continued down the hallway, and my anger toward Rose was temporarily sated at the sight of the grandiose rooms that caused even my bitter jaw to slack. There was a library with floor to ceiling bookshelves filled with old leather volumes. I heard a story once that in the olden days people would pay to have fake books placed between the real ones to fill out their collection, but I got the feeling that Rama would frown on that sort of practice and insist that every book be authentic. Across from the library there was a lounge filled with red and brown leather chairs arranged around a roaring fire, jazz music blaring from a record player.

"Jazz was the one thing humanity got right," he said. "That, and books, of course."

"I couldn't agree more," Rose said, and her voice brought the venom boiling up into my throat.

I bit my tongue as Rama led us past a dining room, a game room, and up the stairs to a landing which broke to the left and right.

"Now," Rama mumbled. "Which way?"

"To the right, sir!" the woman called out.

"Thank you, Maricel!" he yelled back. "I would forget my own head if it wasn't attached." He continued right and stopped at a large white door. "You'll have to forgive me, but I only had one room made up. Given the situation, maybe you would like—"

"It's fine with me," Rose said curtly, turning to me. "If it's okay with Chelle."

It wasn't okay with me. I wanted her gone and I wanted my space, but I wouldn't give her the satisfaction of being the bigger person. "It's fine."

Rama led us inside to a bright, airy room with high ceilings and a large, four-poster bed covered with white sheets and a red, silk awning. Normally, seeing the bed would have excited me, but thinking of sleeping with Rose turned my stomach, which made me even madder, because usually that was all I wanted to do.

"This is our nicest guest room. We call it the white room, for obvious reasons." Aside from the red awning and some gilded accents, everything in the room was white, down to the vanities and curtains. "It's the hardest thing to keep clean, which makes it all the more impressive."

"Why didn't we hide out here?" I asked. "Seems nicer than that dingy bar."

"Polite society wouldn't approve of my dealings with the Circle of Truth, and I have an image to maintain."

"Wasn't your cover blown when they raided the bar earlier?" Rose asked. Even though it was a good question, I wasn't about to give her kudos for it.

"Not at all." Rama pulled a talisman out of his shirt. "This little baby helps hide my face from those I don't want to see it."

I leaned closer to see a vial of red liquid hidden inside the leaf shaped golden locket. "Is that blood?"

He nodded. "A drop for every person who I wish to see my true form. A sacrifice to the goddess of truth, Veritas. It cost me a lot to get a hold of this charm. It is one of the most prized in all of the Celestial Realm."

"Well, isn't that lucky for you," I said, a little too sharply.

Rama must have heard the edge in my voice, because he stepped back to the door. "I'll leave you two alone. Please don't kill each other, and if you need anything, just call for Maricel. This house is enchanted so she can hear her name from anywhere and appear within seconds."

"That must be horrible," I said. "To be forced into service on a whim like that."

He cocked his head. "I never really thought about it."

"Why am I not surprised?"

He didn't answer. When he was gone, Rose sat on the edge of the vanity and traced her foot on the golden florets that cracked across the floor.

"I'm sorry."

I took myself as far across the room from her, sitting on the far end of the bed. "No, you're not."

She sighed. "No, I'm not, but I'm sorry for not being sorry."

I let myself fall backward onto the bed. "I'm going to die, you know, if I help them."

"Don't say things like that," she said. "You don't know that."

I pushed myself up onto my elbows. "Yes, I do. Nox told me I was the key to something, and Rama...he said I was some sort of catalyst; that Nox created me to die at the right time, the final part of her plan."

Rose frowned. "Why didn't you tell me this before?"

"Would it have mattered?"

She stomped toward me. "Of course it would have been different. We have to get you out of here right now."

I chuckled. "Do you really think we can leave? We had our chance to go, and now, we're stuck."

"I don't believe that," Rose said. She grabbed my hand and tried to pull me up. "I saved you from death once, and I have no desire to do it again."

I steadied her hands in mine. "Hey, it's okay. It's okay."

"You can't die. You can't. You just can't." She burst into tears and kept repeating herself.

I stood up and took her into my arms. "It's really hard to be mad at somebody who's crying like this." I thought for a second. "Also, aren't I supposed to be the one crying?"

She nodded into my shoulder. "Yes, why aren't you crying?"

I shrugged. "I've died once, Rose. I mourned my life already. I don't have the energy to do it again."

"If you told me before, I would have left. You know I would have left, right?"

"Honestly, no. I didn't. I hoped you would, but...I don't want you to regret me, Rose. When you said that if we left you would grow bitter of me...I can't have that. I would literally rather die than have that happen."

She squeezed me tighter. "You're not going to die. I'm not going to let that happen."

I don't know why, but I believed her. She spoke with such resolve. This was the girl that rescued me from the Underworld and brought me back to life. I owed everything to her, and if she wanted to save the universe, who was I to argue? Just so long as I got to hold her in my arms.

"I believe you."

"You goddamn better," she said, snuffling. "You better."

CHAPTER 15

NIMUE

Cassandra led me past the ballroom where I had met the King in Yellow and was divested from my skin, to a large dining room filled with every manner of food imaginable. There were what looked like chicken thighs and pork chops, and also eyeballs, blood pudding, and intestine soup.

"Ah, you have arrived, my lovely," Hastur stood, dressed in a yellow, intricately embroidered robe, his face still shrouded in mystery from the hood that covered everything but his glowing red eyes. He floated around the table more than stepped, and laid his gaunt, thin fingers softly on Cassandra's hand. "You have done well, my child."

She couldn't suppress a smile, which caused her lopsided skin to pinch and undulate unnaturally. "Thank you, my liege."

His finger raised to touch her malformed mouth before his voice turned sour. "Now, leave us."

Cassandra didn't say another word. She turned on her heels and walked down the hallway, her footsteps echoing. When she was out of sight, he turned to his banquet and gestured with a sweep of his arm.

"I thought you might be hungry," he said.

I was famished, but I knew better than to show weakness, especially now that I had a reprieve from my pain. "I am a bit peckish."

Hastur guided me around the table toward the seat next to his. "That is not what I heard. My girls say you devour the moldy bread we feed you like a rabid dog. They have told me it is quite pathetic, so I thought a banquet would be more befitting to one of your stature."

He pulled out the chair and I fell into it, my stomach growling its betrayal. "And what do you know of my stature?"

"As much as Cassandra has told me, and I have gleaned. You were once the Queen of Oz, touched by the blessing of Hera and Epiales, along with a host of other accolades, including having come back from the dead to inhabit a new body, a feat even the gods have trouble duplicating."

"A good summary." I nodded slightly. "I have been known to be quite resourceful, and dogged in my determination, when I see something I want."

"And what do you want right now?" Hastur asked.

"The same thing I have always wanted," I replied, buttering a piece of bread, "Everything."

He chuckled lightly. "A woman after my own heart."

I took a bite of the roll and let out an audible moan. I didn't even care, as the taste of grain and gluten filled my mouth. My stomach ached for more. "This is much better than the slop you feed me in the dungeon."

"We eat much better up here. Tell me, how do you feel about your experience in my dungeon?"

"What is this, a Yelp review?" I realized he wouldn't understand that reference, and in fact, I only barely remembered it from my brief time as a waitress. "It was horrible and miserable in equal measure. I could have used a twisted mind like you in Oz. I might have broken more of my prisoners that way."

"And do you feel sufficiently broken?"

My immediate answer was yes, but I restrained myself. "It has certainly shown me that my mistress could not be bothered to come save me, if that was your intention."

"My intention was to give you a chance to think about what you have done, and if that included coming to dislike your mistress, like so many before you, then so be it."

"I see now how you have kept your throne with so many trying to usurp your power."

He nodded slowly, watching me eat. "You are well-versed in the game of royalty, I am sure."

"Yes, you must keep your front and back protected at all times, for there is always somebody coming to stab you."

"And what of me?" Hastur said. "Do you have the same enmity for me that you did when you took up arms against me?"

I snatched up a turkey leg, or what passed for one in Carcosa, and took a bite of it, savoring the juice as it dripped down my chin. "I never held any malice toward you. I was given an assignment and tasked with carrying it out. Nothing more...and as for you ripping the skin from my body—I have done the same to my enemies."

"And are we enemies, Nimue?" the King in Yellow asked. I noticed that he had not taken a bite of food but watched me intently as I did.

"That is entirely up to you, my king," I said. "I am new to this land, and perhaps I was taken astray by Rapunzel and Baba."

"You are an expert diplomat," he said. "I could use

another princess in my ranks as ruthless and cunning as you."

"Is that a job offer?"

"The makings of one. It is too soon to lower my guard to you now, but you have piqued my interest." He stood. "Please stay and finish to your heart's content. I know you are holding back because I am here." He pulled a bell out of his robe and placed it on the table. "When you have eaten your fill, ring this bell and one of my attendants will show you to your new room."

"Room? You're not sending me back to the dungeon?"

He cocked his head. "Not until I know whether to make you suffer, or give you a new life, filled with the type of power even one like you could never imagine." He took another moment to linger over my face, undeterred by my hideous nature. "Cassandra was right about you. I don't think I have ever met your equal."

"Is that a compliment?" I asked.

"None that I would ever admit to, my dear. Until we meet again."

With that, he shuffled out of the room, and when he was gone, I dove into the food, shoving as much of it into my mouth as possible. It was undignified, sure, but it was also glorious.

CHAPTER 16
ARIEL

"Fluctus inpulsa!" I shouted. An explosion of force rippled through the water and loosened Vivian's grip on my arm. *"Cereritas!"*

Before Hypnos bestowed his gift on me, I could barely cast a simple light spell without exhaustion, but now, after two energy-intensive spells, my limbs pulsated as if the magic fed my body.

I shot through the water at a speed I couldn't have hoped to obtain before. "Leave me alone!"

"You can't get away from me!" Vivian shouted.

Even with my increased speed, she was closing in. She belonged there, while I was only a tolerated guest, and she cut through the water with ease. A massive charge of electricity bolted through the deep, missing my ear by inches.

"Are you trying to kill me?" I ducked behind an embankment of coral. "I thought we were sisters."

"Mother told us to bring you to her by any means necessary, and I took that to mean even if you are nothing but a pile of ash."

Vivian and I had a contentious relationship, that much I

knew, but I never knew she had such animosity toward me. In our way, I thought us friends.

"Just let me go, Vivian. I don't want to hurt you."

"Don't worry. You won't." The explosion she sent shook caused a huge chunk of the coral to break off and shatter. "I'm the future queen of the mermaids. Do you think I'm scared of a human?"

"I have been blessed by Hypnos. My power is like nothing you have ever seen! *Rota aqua!*" I screamed, unleashing a water wheel spinning hungrily toward Vivian.

She dispelled it before it could touch her. "Your power has grown, but you are still only human."

She clapped her hands together, and the sea shook under me, breaking the coral in two and forcing me to scramble away. Pluming hot water spewed from the cracked ground and scalded my arms and legs, forcing me from my hiding spot.

I knew I was close to the cave, but Vivian's attacks threw me off course and I lost my exact position. *"Nox inveniat in spelunca."*

A red light shot from my hands and I followed it. For the moment, it looked like I had lost Vivian, but I had no sooner thought those words than she blew past me, knocking me hard in the stomach and spinning me back into the depths.

"You can't lose me. When will you realize that? Give up, and I will kill you quickly."

"Why do you hate me so much? I have never been anything but nice to you."

"And it's so tiring. You are the golden child that my mother holds us all up to." She closed her fist, and a piece of broken coral crashed into me. "Do you know what it means to be compared unfavorably to a mongrel like you?" Another rock of coral smashed into me. "I can't tell you how many days I dreamt of exiling you from my kingdom when I was queen, and letting the mermaids have their way with you."

"I'm sorry you feel that way," I said, heaving, with cuts up and down my legs. "But it's not my fault you were never good enough for Ursula." I whipped my hands out and clapped them together. "*Iactare petram!*"

The pieces of rock that had smashed against me suspended for a moment before firing back at Vivian. Her eyes went wide as she was pelted with a dozen small pieces of rock, sending her spiraling.

"*Flagellum aqua!*" I screamed, the water around me parted and formed into a whip that I swung at her, slapping her into the ocean floor, once, twice, three times, before the water condensed back around us. I held my hand out to a large boulder. "*Motus!*"

The earth quaked and the boulder cut in two, falling onto my sister's broken body. I didn't want to see what would happen to her, so I turned away. She had been in my life for as long as I could remember.

"You are pathetic!" Vivian screeched after me. "You don't even have the stomach to finish the job!"

I turned in time to see the boulder hurtling toward me, and I could barely push the water around me to slow it down before it slammed into me. When I finally came to a stop, the boulder had me pinned down to a crack in the ocean floor between two jagged pieces of coral.

Vivian's orange body bolted toward me, but there was something else in the deep. It was the small red dot that I had sent to locate Nox's cave. If I could only get there, I could cause a rockslide and give myself some time to search for clues.

"*Vitae,*" I growled, placing my hands under the rock.

After a moment of pressing against it, it came free, and I pulled out my mangled leg. I used whatever speed I had left to kick away but I barely made it to the edge of the cavern before Vivian was on top of me. *"Ruina!"*

The cavern collapsed, closing me inside. I didn't know how I would escape the cave when I had finished and needed to make it back to the surface, but that was future me's problem. Escaping from Vivian was the most important thing at the moment.

Vivian cried out as the rocks tumbled over her, and when they finally slowed, her hand still reached through. I watched as she quieted and it fell limp.

CHAPTER 17

ROSE

Rama didn't disturb us the rest of the day. Either he was busy or he recognized that Chelle and I needed our space to deal with the issues that had weaseled into our relationship. Even after we resolved our fight, we spent hours talking about the future, and past, and trying to come to an agreement about what to do next.

"Are you sure that you're on board with this?" I asked when we had finally crawled to bed, exhausted both by our daring escape earlier in the day, and the grueling emotional labor of trying to fix the rifts in our relationship. "I know my path, but you don't have to walk it with me."

"No, I'm not sure," Chelle replied. "But I think you're right. Unless we fix this, we'll be fighting our entire lives, and we'll never feel safe."

We had been together again for months back on Earth, but we were so busy—really, I was so busy—that we never truly sat down and understood just how much we had grown, both up and apart, over the past years. Chelle was a different person, after dying and becoming a Fate, than when we were simple college students; I had become a queen, been blessed by two gods, and led an army of fairies against Nimue before becoming the unwilling spokesperson for all magical beings. Still, for both of us, it seemed we expected the same person to exist in our memory than the ones we had grown into over our adventures.

I kissed Chelle on the forehead. "You should get some sleep."

"I don't sleep much," she murmured. "But I am exhausted somehow."

She closed her eyes, and I let her snakes rest across my chest. The last two weeks felt like a fairy tale, a vacation from reality where we refused to acknowledge the elephant in the room—are the people we became the kind of people we still wanted to be with? I would be lying if I didn't see Chelle as a damsel in distress for me to save, nor that she saw me as the same. We had shrunk into two-dimensional people in each other's minds, but we had hopes and dreams, just like we always had before, except they were different from the ones we once shared.

Once Chelle was asleep, I slid out of bed and put on a night gown that Maricel had hanging in our closets. I chose the pink, silk one, leaving the powder blue for Chelle, and snuck out of the room.

It didn't take long to find Rama, who was sitting in a high-back red leather chair in his lounge. A book rested in his lap while he stared at the fire, idly swirling a glass of brandy.

"Can we talk?" I asked, and it jolted him from his daze.

"Of course," he said. "Have you resolved things with your paramour yet?"

"I think so. It's hard. Even though we've been together for the past couple of years, it doesn't feel that way. We've spent more time pining for each other than actually being together."

He nodded. "It is the way with long distance. You grow into different people, and when you meet again, you're almost like strangers."

It pained me to agree with him. "You're right. There is a piece of Chelle that I recognize, but it's buried under layers that I don't. I want so desperately to unearth it all, but I'm worried I won't like what I find."

"The same thing happened with my darling Kadlu, the only woman who ever captured even a piece of my heart."

"I can imagine that with the length of your lives, and the fact you can travel to an endless array of planets, that long distance would be hard."

He swallowed, and a pained look flashed across his face. "So very hard. We were apart for nearly a decade, and when we came back together, neither of us liked the god we had become." He sighed. "I have regretted letting her go every day since, and now you must make the difficult choice whether to fall in love with the person Chelle is now, or accept that growing apart is a part of life and say your goodbyes."

"I have already decided that even though she is different from the woman I fell in love with, she is even more amazing now."

"Good, good," he said. "But just know, if you survive this, she will change again, and you might not recognize that woman, either. Love is constantly falling in love with the person your partner becomes, every day, for the rest of your lives."

"I can't wait to fall in love with every woman she becomes for the rest of her life."

He took a sip of brandy and pointed to me with the

glass still in his hand. "To me, that is true love, being willing to fall in love with the same person, over and over again, while they become new versions of themselves until the end of time."

I sat down in the chair beside his. "We have decided to help you, but what Chelle told me—" I gathered myself. "She cannot die. I don't care about Nox's plan. No matter what, you have to protect Chelle with every bit of your being. She cannot die. Do you understand?"

"I swear she will not die by my hand or my actions."

I shook my head. "That's not good enough. I have been around you gods enough to know that you will twist anything to your advantage. I need you to make a magical pact with me." I held out my hand. "*Magicis foedus.*"

"This is a little excessive," Rama said, looking at my outstretched hand. "I am a man of my words."

"You are not a man at all," I said. "And you have seen more than me. Because of that, you know more than me, and thus can manipulate me in ways I cannot imagine. This is the only way I can be sure you will be honest."

"If this will get you to help me, I will gladly make this pact with you." He set his drink down and placed his hand in mine.

"Repeat after me." I cleared my throat. "I swear on my eternal life that I will take no action that will put Rose or Chelle's life in danger and will do my utmost best to save them if they are in danger. Should I fail to do so, I forfeit my immortal life, and will walk among the mortals, and die as they do."

"You don't want me to die if I betray you?"

"You will die, but I think that for a god, losing your faculties and your vigor, slowly, over a mortal life, is the worst punishment I can imagine."

"I was mortal once, you know?"

I stared at him. "Is there a reason you won't repeat my words?"

"No," he replied. "I just wanted to make sure you understood—"

"Then say the words." I repeated them, watching the fear swell in his eyes. Whatever gambit he was planning, however he was going to betray us, was clicking around behind his eyes. Finally, he bowed his head and repeated the words. An orange wisp of light wrapped around us both and seared itself into our skin, down to the bone.

When it was finished, Rama pulled his hand back and rubbed it. "And what happens if you betray me?"

"Please," I said with a smile. "If I wanted to betray you, I would walk out that door and you would never see me again. The fact I'm still here is proof that I won't do that. I just had to be sure we were both on the same page, since I know how little human lives mean to the gods."

"That might be true in aggregate, but I can assure you, your lives mean a great deal to all of us."

"I hope that is true, for your sake." I walked out of the room. "Now, if you'll excuse me. I'm going to enjoy the last hours with my Chelle before we have to separate yet again because of some godly bullshit."

CHAPTER 18
NIMUE

After eating so little for so long, my stomach had shrunk. Stuffing myself with food expanded it so quickly I thought it might burst.

"Are you ready to be taken to your room?"

I looked up to find Delilah, sans her black crown, but with the same alabaster skin, cracked with a glowing green that highlighted the stencils of the forest across her face and body.

I stood up with a groan, holding my stomach. This was pain in a different way than I had felt in the dungeon, and part of me thought that was Hastur's plan all along, to let me torture myself by gorging on too much food. It would have been a devious thing, and the exact kind of thing that his sick mind would come up with.

"Thank you, and yes," I said.

"Then follow me," Delilah growled. It was obvious she thought guiding me through the castle was beneath her. "You have been provided a room adequate for one of your station."

I followed her down the hall. "And what station is that?"

"Former queen, I have heard, and blessed by the gods." She stopped and looked at me. "Or did you think I meant the ragged condition that you find yourself in now?"

"I—I don't know what to think," I said.

"That is for the best," she said. "The more you think you know in this place, the more it can be weaponized against you. My advice is to leave your attachments and preconceptions at the front gate. That is the only way to survive."

"That is the way you survived, then?"

Delilah turned to the same stairwell Hastur had descended during our first meeting in the ballroom. Her hand glided on the black metal railing as she moved slowly from one stair to the next.

"That is how we have all survived." She paused to study me. "It was not long ago that I was laid low like you."

I looked down at my mangled body. The muscles on my legs twitched, sliding together and apart with my steps. "He made you a monster, too."

She held up her hand, twisting it to show off the green trees and brushes traced through her skin. "Do you not find me monstrous now?"

I raised my eyebrows. "I find you glorious, in fact. Powerful, and seductive. When Baba—when I was made to resemble you, for the first time in my life I felt like I was in the body I was meant for."

A small smile cracked her face. "Perhaps you will fit in here after all."

"Will I ever get my skin back?" I asked. "Do you think?"

"It is best not to think about it. Hastur's whims change by the hour. He might come to you tonight and grant you his bounty, or he might keep you like this for a hundred epochs. Even if he chooses to give you some of your beauty back, he can reclaim it just as quickly. All of this is at his behest."

At the top of the staircase, she brushed away a yellow and black curtain that led into a hallway full of twisted black sculptures. A red light flickered above them, creating haunting shadows that seemed to skitter about me as we passed.

"That sounds difficult," I said. "To live in a world like that, I mean."

"As long as you stay on his good side." Delilah cleared her throat, but her eyes were watery, and belied her strong visage. "It is not so bad."

I heard the warble of her words and responded, "You don't sound confident."

"It depends on how malleable you are. Hastur likes girls he can mold, though I believe he likes girls he can break and snap even more."

"Which were you?"

"I was a brittle girl, stubborn. Hastur took great pleasure in breaking me apart and putting me back together, only to smash me apart again. Still does." A tear fell down her cheek. She wiped it away and snarled. "He has no respect for weakness, but it is that weakness on which he feeds."

"I am not weak. He will find strength enough to match him."

She cackled at this. "The only thing he loves more than brittle little things are strong ones that he can melt down and reforge into his perfect creations." She struck a pose like a Parisian model. "Like me, his greatest work of art."

"You make it sound so horrible, but you seem to love it, too."

Another small smile crawled across her face. "That is the difficulty of this life. Incredible power and beauty, but fear and brutality enough for—" She bit her lip. "I have said too much. Again, you will be happy here, so long as you follow instructions."

She turned a corner and came to a long, black door, knobby and overgrown with vines. She pushed on it to reveal a room furnished completely in black, from the wardrobe to the bed sheets. Gothic statues speckled the room, and all the furniture seemed to be carved with similar gargoyles and monsters.

"I will let you get settled." She walked over to the vanity and picked up a bottle of black ichor. "You must drink a swig of this potion every twelve hours to keep away the pain. If you forget..."

"I won't."

A horrible scream came from one of the statues. "Delilah, I have need of you in my chamber."

A shiver went up her spine. "I have to go."

I grabbed her hand. "Wait, please—"

She ripped her hand away, her face vicious. "You have no idea what would happen if I don't. There is one rule, and that is whatever Hastur asks of you, do it without question. If you want to survive here, you would do well to learn it."

With that she stormed out and slammed the door, leaving me alone in a gothic nightmare, wondering if I would have been better off in the dungeon, far away from Hastur's gaze.

CHAPTER 19

CHELLE

Rose rustled me awake when she came back to bed. I wrapped my arms around her and settled on her stomach. "You went to talk to Rama, even though we agreed to let it be."

"I had to know he wasn't going to betray you."

"How did it go?"

"He agreed to a magical pact," she said, rubbing her forearm. "Wasn't happy about it, but he agreed."

"Then at least we know he's not going to betray us, intentionally at least."

"He's just one of them, though. I doubt Hepit, iNyanga, Aditi, or Nox would be so accommodating, especially if Nox's plan was to sacrifice you. If any of them talk to the Board we could be in serious trouble. We're not out of the woods yet."

"Babe, we haven't even entered the woods yet. Let's think about it tomorrow," I said. "Did you find any Ambien?"

Rose shook her head. "No, but I've been sleeping okay here, even if I can't slip into the Dream Realm."

"It's probably for the best. You're already pulled into one realm's drama. You don't need Queen Aine sending you on some crazy mission, too."

Rose yawned. "You're right."

Albie nuzzled on her chest, and I felt her petting him. "We can still leave, you know. The more I think about it, the more dangerous it seems. How did I save three realms and I'm just thinking about it now?"

"Adrenaline, man. It's a crazy drug," she replied and yawned again. "I need some sleep."

I waited until her heartbeat fell into a slow rhythm, and her hand fell from Albie's head before I slipped out of the room. While I was happy that Rose got her conscience clear by talking to Rama, I had something I needed to talk to him about that needed to be kept a secret, at least for a little while. If she could have a heart-to-heart with him, then so could I.

"Were you waiting for me?" I asked him when I found him in the parlor.

"Partially, but you also have very loud feet, unlike your paramour. I heard you coming halfway across the house."

"I have flat feet. It sucks."

"I assume you need something," he said.

I nodded. "I figure that since we're both a couple of needy bitches, I can ask you for a favor."

He rubbed his arm. "I already bound myself to Rose's spell. I don't know how many favors I have left in me."

"Well, since you are trying to kill me, I think you can do one more for me." I looked at the surprise on his face. "And please don't insult me by saying you aren't trying to kill me."

"I wasn't going to deny it," Rama said. "This binding

was a very good idea, though. There's nothing I hate more than the idea of becoming a mortal."

"Becoming a mortal *again*, you mean." I smirked at him. "Rose has a more naïve take on the whole situation, but I'm sure you'll find a way to carry through on your plans for me anyway. I know how much you believe in Nox's vision."

He gave me a level stare before saying, "I'm glad we can be honest with each other. I hate subversion."

This time I outright laughed. "I don't believe that for a second."

"That is your right," he said, swirling his glass. "So, what is it that you need from me?"

"I need some way to communicate with Rose while we're apart from each other," I said.

"That's not something I can—"

"You are a god! Figure it out!" I took a breath and then spoke more softly. "If we are going to be apart from each other, I need to be able to talk to her."

"Something like that could be used by our enemies to destroy us, to trace back—"

"I don't care." I stared at him until he blinked. "Make it happen."

"Perhaps I do have something." He thought for a moment. "Do you like jewelry?"

"Not especially, but I'm not picky if it keeps me in contact with Rose."

"I have just the thing." He walked across the room and opened a small box on his desk, pulling out a red jeweled necklace and an accompanying ring. "This is a set I have treasured for a long time."

"The rubies are a nice touch."

"Rubies? Please, I would never deal with something so pedestrian. These are dragon fire gems, the rarest in the cosmos, made from the fires born at the origin of the universe."

He placed the set in my hand. They were lighter than I imagined. In fact, it felt like nothing was there. "How do they work?"

"One of you wears the ring, and the other the necklace. When you look into them, you can see what the other sees." He grabbed the necklace and twisted it. We disappeared and reappeared in the same spot. "If you twist the necklace, or spin the ring, you can reappear in front of the other person. It's called 'The Heartstring charm,' but be careful with it because once you use it once, you cannot just transport back. It's meant to bring you together, and only for that purpose. I once was intending to give it to my beloved, before...well, now I offer it to you and your beloved. May you have better luck with them than I did."

"Thank you, Rama." I stared at the ring and necklace in my hand. "This is almost sweet."

"It's the least I can do. I am trying to kill you, after all."

"And there it is." I turned to the door. "Goodnight, Rama."

"Goodnight, Chelle. Rest well. We'll work on saving the universe tomorrow."

CHAPTER 20

RED

Zeus's console buzzed to life, and the servers blinked and hummed. The blue aura of Nox's soul oozed out of the box and filled the console with a bright blue glow before descending into the tubes and snaking across the floor. The electrodes attached to Nox's body pulsated, causing her head and chest to twitch in the same rhythm.

"Stop it!" I shouted. "You're going to hurt her!"

Athena grabbed me by the shoulders and dug her fingers into me until I fell to my knees. "Don't act like you care! This goddess treated you like her personal pet, and you don't even know the half of it."

I pulled all my energy together and elbowed her in the stomach. The surprise of it caused her to loosen my grip and I wriggled free. I stood and rushed to the table, but a sudden gust of wind from Zeus blew me backward and I slammed against the far wall.

"Control your prisoner, Athena!"

I righted myself just as she pulled me to my feet and held me tightly to her hip. No matter what I tried, all I could do from that point was watch in horror as the blue aura of the soul slid through the tube and into Nox's body. When it had fully immersed itself inside of her, she let out a horrible scream, and the machine fell silent.

"Lovely," Zeus said. "Let us see how we've done."

"This is the best part," Athena whispered to me.

Zeus walked over to the slab and smiled at Nox. "Hello, my dear Nox. How do you feel?"

Nox's eyes opened, and she let out a groan. "The very last thing I wanted to see when I opened my eyes was your face, so I guess as well as can be expected, given the circumstances."

"Hrm." Zeus's face turned down, disappointed. "That's not very polite. Don't you have anything nice to say about me?"

"I don't think so but let me check." Nox thought for a moment. "Tell me, do you know the horror of having your soul pulled from your body, dear cousin?"

"I can only imagine it would be as horrible as being reunited with your body is wonderful."

"It was awful, dear Zeus. It was as if every one of my nerve endings had been burned off at once, and still, I would take that a thousand times over spending another second with you. That is the nicest thing I have to say about you."

"I'm sorry you feel that way." He tsked. "You are obstinate to the end. I really thought we had cracked it this time."

"Let me at her, sir," Athena said. "I'll make her talk."

"Hold your temper, Athena, though I do appreciate your vigor, as always." He turned back to Nox. "I would like to know what you plan to do with this human, and the others that you turned from souls into this creature of pure energy. Are you compelled to tell me the truth?"

Nox's eyes narrowed. "There is absolutely nothing in the universe that would make me tell you that, Zeus, and I can't believe you would have the audacity to ask—no, that is not true. I can absolutely believe that you would have the audacity. After all, you are a pompous windbag."

"A pity," Zeus said, and without another word he slammed his hand into Nox's chest and pulled out her soul, throwing it back into its prison. Nox didn't fight, or squirm. She grimaced for a moment, and then fell backward, jaw slack, and eyes vacant. Zeus walked back to his desk and placed the soul box inside his desk, locking it carefully.

"That was disappointing." He waved us away. "I would like to be alone now."

"And what about this one?" Athena said.

"I will have need of her later." His voice was low, dejected, almost as if he had the capacity for emotion. "For now, take her back to her cell."

Athena pushed me towards the door. I took one last look at Zeus before we left, a piteous figure, far from the blustering, confident god that had strutted through the room when I arrived.

CHAPTER 21
NIMUE

After Delilah left, I tried the door and found that it was unlocked. Since the entire castle was a horror show, and only absolutely insane people would willingly wander the halls, it wasn't so surprising.

I creaked open the door and stepped out into the hall. It might have been the stuff of horrors, but it was likely my only chance to escape. Perhaps Baba would be forgiving, since I had been betrayed by one of Rapunzel's operatives. Even if not, I trusted her to be kinder than the King in Yellow.

"I wouldn't do that if I were you," I heard a raspy voice say to me. I turned around and found another of Hastur's princesses, pure white skin with six horns protruding from her head. She sat, leaning backward on a short stool. "At least, not without your ichor bottle."

"Oh," I said, trying to feign confusion and cursing that I would forget something so important to keep me out of pain. "I was just trying to get my bearings."

She stood. "Now, I'm not saying I don't believe you, but I am saying that you're a liar. You're not the first who has tried to take this opportunity to escape, and I can tell you from personal experience that it is a bad idea."

"What did he do to you when you tried to escape?"

She sucked her teeth for a long moment. "He hung me upside down and let his mongrel dogs nibble on my face. When I thought they had their fill, he eviscerated me and allowed them to feast on my bowels." The woman lightly touched her stomach, as if it were a reflex. "And when I thought maybe sweet death would take me, he healed me, and forced me to go through it again and again."

"That's horrible," I said. "I'm sorry for you."

"Don't be." She shrugged. "It's nothing like what he has done to you."

Her clear white eyes reflected me back to myself, but there was a deep wound in them as well; to all of the princesses. When I met them at the party, I saw them as ice cold, but how else could they be any different, given what Hastur had done to them.

"We don't have to compare our scars, especially when they were both given by the same man."

"I wouldn't say he is a man, per se. A man has emotion, needs, and desires. The only thing I have ever seen Hastur desire is to watch others in pain. Everything else is just a precursor to that end."

I knew then the truth of the meal Hastur left for me. "I thought it might have been kindness Hastur showed when he left me alone with a feast." I pulled at my stomach, which still felt like it was going to rip in half. "But judging by what you are saying, likely he just wanted me to suffer at my own hand."

"It is one of his favorite methods of torture, to watch his victim hoist themselves on their own petard. He says that when a person is the bearer of their own doom, the suffering is all the more delicious."

"I have done a lot of sick things in my time, but that is horrible."

The woman stepped forward, her eyes glinting. "You have not even seen a fraction of his power. He feeds not on food, but on the suffering of his people. The more they suffer, the more powerful he becomes."

"I have never met one, but I know of many demons and vile creatures who feed off the pain of others. Hastur—"

She covered my mouth with a shaking hand. After several seconds of listening, she dropped her hand. "If you know what is good for you, stop saying his name out loud. His name is charmed, and he can hear any who speak it. It seems he is busy with my sister, so we are safe for now. Be careful even to think his name, for it could cause him to appear, and it is better when his gaze is off of you completely."

"I will remember this kindness, sister."

"You should hope that we do not become sisters. It is a fate worse than death."

"It doesn't have to be," I whispered. "You are powerful on your own. You and your sisters can rise up and take him down." Cassandra had led me to believe I could bend the sisters to my will and unite them against Hastur. If she was wrong, or I was wrong to take her advice, then I was in for a world of suffering, but so would I be if I was made a princess.

"Others of us have tried. If you think our fates are terrible, you should see theirs."

"But if we succeed, this horror will end forever."

"It is a nice thought, but the king keeps my sisters and I at war with each other for his affections. We would never come together for something like that and would end up eating each other alive in the process."

"If I could bring you together, would you be with me, when the time comes?"

She thought for a long moment, then nodded. "If you could, then yes. I would be with you."

This could have been another of the king's tricks, but I had already dug my hole. The only hope was to keep digging and hope I could find salvation in the depths.

"Thank you. I'm sorry, sister...please tell me your name. I've forgotten it after all the torture."

She nodded. "I forgot the one I was born with, but the king gave me the name Elvira. It bristles my skin every time I hear it."

"I will make this right, sister, if it is the last thing I do."

"It just might be the last thing you do, Nimue. I hope it is not, for your sake. This is the first glimmer of hope I have had in some time."

CHAPTER 22
ROSE

I had not been able to break through to the Dream Realm without medication for months, but the sleep I fell into after I returned to the room must have been deep, because almost instantly I found myself in the Wild Bill Saloon and Casino. The entire gambling district of Urgu was newly created and tacky, based on Hypnos's love for Reno.

I hated its gaudiness something fierce and would never have chosen to appear there on my own, which was how I knew I had been summoned there by a powerful force. Sure enough, through the smoke and the musk of gamblers who hadn't bathed in days, Hypnos sat at a Blackjack table, his pink eyes trained on me. With a quick motion of his hand, he beckoned me over.

"Are you okay?" he asked when I slid next to him.

"Of course not," I snarled. "This whole situation is bonkers, and we've been dropped into the middle of it yet again to clean up your mess, woefully unprepared and without even half the information we need to fix things. I am a lot of things, but okay is not even close to one of them."

"Fair enough."

"I'm surprised to see you. I thought Zeus would have ripped you in half."

"He tried." Hypnos smiled. "Being the god of dreams has its advantages. Before he delivered the killing blow, I slipped into the dreams of one of the unconscious prisoners, and then, well, sometimes being the warden to a prison fortified by the gods has its advantages. This place is teetering on the brink of collapse, but I have, as of yet, been able to keep Zeus and his minions out. Still, it is only a matter of time before the wards fail and they come for me."

"Where will you go?"

He shook his head. "I have lived too long to run again, which is why I have a vested interest in seeing you succeed."

"I thought maybe you would want to save your mother."

"I didn't say it was the only reason." He smiled. "Now, I can see you have about a hundred questions and very little time, so how about we cut to the heart of it."

"Sounds good to me." My eyes narrowed. "How much do you know about what's going on?" I wanted to exclude him from joining our cause.

"Enough to know you're in a world of trouble." He glanced at the dealer. "Hit."

The dealer flipped over a 6, making Hypnos's 15 an even 21. "Twenty-one." He flipped over a card. "And the dealer busts. Well played, sir."

"Do you really get any enjoyment knowing you are always going to win?" I asked.

He frowned. "Why would you play a game you can't win?

"Isn't that part of the fun, the uncertainty?"

"Would you fight a war without knowing whether you would win or lose?" His rolled his eyes. "Never mind, I already know the answer to that question in your case."

I sighed. "It's not a war."

He snapped his fingers, and everything else disappeared except for the two of us, sitting across from each other, in a white room. "So, you aren't trying to take on the whole Board, and working with the Circle of Truth to do it?"

"How could you possibly know that?"

He tapped his temple. "It helps to be the god of dreams sometimes. I've learned a few tricks over the years, so yeah, I can burrow into people's memories and learn their intentions."

I sat straight up. "You haven't told anyone else, have you?"

"Of course not. The Board arrested my mother and they've been after control of the Dream Realm for as long as it's existed. One thing myself and my dear departed brother could agree on is our deep, resting hatred for Zeus and his ilk. Nothing would make me happier than taking them down a few hundred pegs."

"Does that mean you'll help us, then?"

"Not officially. If the Board ever found out, well, that would be all they needed to strip me of my realm." He leaned back. "Besides, I have no love for Rama, either. He always humored my mother and led her down this foolish path of ruin in the first place."

"I thought that this whole thing was Nox's plan."

"Not at first. She has always fomented insurrection against Zeus and the Board, but it wasn't until she met Rama that it became an obsession. I was always able to temper my mother's hot head, but after my brother banished me to Earth, needless to say my absence allowed her to radicalize even further."

"I'm sorry to hear that," I replied, taking this in. "In fairness, I don't trust him at all."

"Good." Hypnos clenched his fists. "You always have a friend in Urgu, Rose, but I caution you against trusting Rama. He is a conniving shitweasel who lusts for power. Even if he masks it with noble intentions, just remember that somebody has to pick up the pieces in the Board's demise, and by leading the charge against them, he is positioning himself as the natural choice."

"I won't let that happen."

"I believe in you, Rose. I never had much hope in humanity, except a fool's hope. Just remember that Rama is eternal, and while I cannot discern the depths of his plan, I can only tell you never to let down your guard."

"That's good advice, no matter which god you are dealing with." I smiled at him. "I appreciate your concern. If you think of anything else, let me know."

"As long as you remember to sleep, I will find and watch over you. Count on it."

I laid my hand on top of his. "Thank you for trying so hard to protect me."

"Of course, my dear. I don't just go giving my blessing out willy-nilly." He looked up. "And now, I'm sorry to say, but we must say goodbye. One final parting piece of advice: When you meet Kadlu, be honest with her, no matter what Rama tells you."

"I always find honesty is the best policy."

CHAPTER 23
ARIEL

No, no, no. I just wanted to stop Vivian, not kill her. I locked my hands around her exposed arm. "Come on, come on!"

I yanked hard, but she didn't budge. The rocks were unstable, crumbling if I so much as looked at them wrong, and with every movement of my body, the rocks groaned, threatening to topple down upon me, but I couldn't stop. Vivian's death would throw the mermaid kingdom into flux, and, more personally, I had a deep love for my false sister, even if she had just tried to kill me.

"*Fluctus inpulsa!*" I shouted. A shock wave burst forth and cracked across the rock face. The spell came with more power the second time I shouted it, bursting some of the boulders into the sea beyond. I tried again to move Vivian. I knew she was alive, because otherwise she would have turned to dust, mixing with the salt water to create a murky brine.

I dove back in and tried to yank her free. While I made more progress, it wasn't enough. "*Ut gravibus pluma,*" I muttered, and the rocks glowed a faint green and slid away.

I wrenched her from her rocky prison. Her eyes were

swollen shut and her lip had puffed to twice its size. Black bruises dabbled her strong body, making her look as weak as I often felt around her. Most alarming was the dark, bruised ring around her throat.

"Vivian? Can you hear me?" My voice cracked. I wasn't a healer, but if I could cause her such pain, then I had to try and fix it as well.

"*Sana,*" I whispered under my breath as I touched my sister's cold, scaly skin. My hands glowed a bright white and pulsated. "*Sarcio.*"

Her bruises began to shrink, replaced by the bright orange that signaled her royal bloodline. I moved my hands up her body to her neck and wrapped my hands around it. The crushing bruise that covered her windpipe disappeared, and Vivian coughed, then heaved violently, flailing her arms.

"Easy," I said, guiding her down to the floor of the cave.

When her breathing calmed, she grabbed my hand, squeezing tightly. Her face was still fattened with bruises. "What are you doing?"

"I'm trying to save your life."

"After you nearly killed me? Why would you do such a thing?"

"I'm not trying to kill you. You were attacking me. I had to defend myself, but regardless of how you feel about me, I still love you."

"You speak of love, and it makes you weak."

"Love does not make you weak. It makes you strong to love something outside of yourself. You wouldn't know that, of course."

She slid away from me. "I care for my people. It is a responsibility that you would never understand."

"I am here trying to save the whole Dream Realm. That

includes your people, by the way, and you decided it was better to kill me than help."

She fell against the wall of the cave and sighed. "Perhaps my rage blinded me."

"You think?"

"What does Nox have to do with all of this?"

"I don't know yet. That's why I'm here, to figure out if there are any clues that can help me find Rapunzel's left eye."

"I don't know what that is." She shook her head. "It sounds disgusting."

"I haven't thought about it much, but okay, yeah, it does."

Vivian dropped her head. "I know of a vault where Nox keeps her most precious objects. If you heal my face, I will guide you to it."

I pursed my lips. "This isn't a trap, is it?"

Her expression turned hard enough that she winced. "If there is one thing you should know about me, it's that I will always stab you in the front."

"That is true. You are a terrible liar."

"It would have made my life easier to accept you, and yet, I could not do so, and I never hid my feelings about your kind, even though it angered my mother. Is that not true?"

I nodded. "Even though it hurt me greatly, you never treated me like an equal."

"Because you are not my equal. However, if you are truly here to help my people, then I owe you my allegiance until such time our goals diverge."

"They are my people, too."

"No, they are not." Vivian's words were matter of fact. "That is yet another lie Ursula has told you. Do not believe her forked tongue, and always listen for the words coming from the side of her mouth."

"I believe you," I said. "But please know that my power has grown, as you have seen, and if you betray me, I will take you down."

"You lack the killer instinct. If you had it, then I would already be dead."

"I don't have to kill you to make your life miserable. You should know that better than anyone, since you've been making mine a nightmare for years."

"Touché, Ariel." She pressed her hand to her chest. "Perhaps I underestimated you. Now, please make me beautiful again."

I smiled at her. "That assumes you were beautiful in the first place, sister."

CHAPTER 24

RED

Athena threw me once again into my darkened cell, with nothing for comfort but the thoughts in my head. I desperately needed for Rama to be okay, and for him to answer me.

"Rama," I whispered, closing my eyes, though the cell was dark enough that I couldn't much tell the difference. "Please."

There was silence for a long moment before I heard his voice again in my head. "Gabrielle? Oh, thank the lords you are still alive."

"Rama!" A big smile crested on my face, and I remembered to lower my voice. "You're alive."

"And so are you. I was worried about you. When I tried to contact you, your mind was locked to me. Where have you been?" I told him everything that had happened since I left my cell. "Ah, yes. They keep the Sanctuary well-guarded from all attacks, including psionic ones."

"What are we going to do about Nox?" I asked, my voice wavering at the memory of what Zeus put her through.

"I'm working on it. It might not seem true, but Zeus's

actions are very encouraging. It shows he is not as far along as we feared, and that even though he has Nox's body and soul, he cannot force her to give away her secrets. I hope our luck extends to iNyanga and the others."

"I'm glad you can see the good in this whole thing."

"Are you kidding, Gabrielle? You have met with Zeus and lived. Do you know how few mortals can say the same?"

"But I am trapped in this cell, completely helpless."

"You might think that is true, but you have much power. In fact, the Board is so enamored with that power that they will keep trying to use it for their own gain. You are a grain of sand in their perfect machine, and they will do anything to suss it out before you bring the whole thing to a grinding halt."

"Then why wouldn't they just kill me if I'm such a nuisance?"

"Because they need to understand the part you play first. As long as the reason for your creation remains obscure to them, we can use it to our advantage." Rama stopped for a moment. "There are things you will see soon that will make you doubt me, so I must beg for your trust."

"You got me imprisoned and lost Nox. In what way do you deserve my trust?"

"I don't deserve it, but I must have it. Otherwise, everything else breaks down. I am devising a way to save you and Nox and bring you to safety, but it means doing things I will not be proud of."

"I have been in that position before." I couldn't very well deny him when he was my best chance for freedom, not while he still held sway over Rose. "Very well. I have no other choice but to trust you, after all. My only other choice is to go it alone, and I think that might have me stuck in the darkness for a long time."

"I'm glad to hear that. I will get you out of there, Gabrielle. Believe that, if for no other reason than you are an integral part of Nox's plan. Even if everything you have said is simply lip service, please at least know to defeat the Board, we need you alive."

It wasn't much comfort, but knowing I was important meant that people would be looking to save me. It also meant I was a valuable bargaining chip in the game the gods were playing, so I needed to keep my wits about me. I didn't know what Rama meant to do that he was so insistent on my trust, but the thought of it turned my stomach. Gods did not operate on the same morality that humanity did, so something that chaffed even his moral compass was something I didn't care to see.

"We are with you," Rama said. "And we do not abandon our own."

"Thank you, Rama. I am with you, too."

CHAPTER 25

CHELLE

I heard Rose moan and her hands stretched out into the air after hours staring into the ceiling. As she wrapped her arms around me, her engagement ring glinted in the light. "Good morning, my love. How did you sleep?"

"Uneasily, as always," I replied. Why was I so nervous? She had already said yes once before, and even though we were engaged, the thought of dropping to one knee and saying the words filled me with terror.

Rose's fingers slid up my chest toward my neck, where she felt the dragon fire necklace that Rama had given me. "Is this new?" She sat up and looked at it. "It's nice. I like it."

"Yeah, Rama gave it to me."

She popped up straight. "When did you talk to Rama?"

"Ummm...after you went back to bed, I got thirsty and went to get a drink."

"Hrm," she replied. "Are you feeling okay? You seem a little jittery."

She placed her head on my forehead, even though she must have known I couldn't get sick, not since Nox brought me back. I pulled back from her and leapt from the bed. "I'm fine. It's just…"

Rose cocked her head to one side then the other. "What's wrong? You're scaring me."

"I—" I took a breath. "I love you, Rose."

She giggled. "I love you, too, silly. Is that really what you are so worried about? I know we had a fight, but of course I still love you."

I felt my pocket, where the dragon fire ring rested. I wrapped it around my fingers. "You don't understand." My eyes fell to the engagement ring she twisted on her finger. "Well, you probably do, but I'm going to say it anyway. I don't like people, Rose, never have. Every time I opened myself to people, they let me down. Everyone, except for you."

"Well, that's not true. I mean, literally yesterday—"

"You didn't have to save me," I said, ignoring her. "But you did. You literally saved me from Hell. I owe you every-thing—my life, my universe, my existence…my very soul is yours." I took her hands, preventing her from twisting the ring one more rotation. "Can I borrow that ring for a second?"

"Why would you—oh—" A smile grew on her face as if she knew what I was about to do. "Oh! Yeah, sure." She pulled her ring off her finger. "You really don't have to do this. I already—"

"I want to, okay? You deserve the very best, and the least I can do—" She placed the ring in my hand. "Okay, so I had this whole thing planned. I was going to charter a boat and take you out into the middle of the sea, where we could see the Statue of Liberty and the skyline." I stopped and swallowed loudly. "But that seemed impractical, given your schedule. Then I was going to slide the ring across the table while we ate a quiet meal, but even that was messed up by the gods—they really screw up so much."

Rose placed her hand on either side of my face. "Focus."

"Right," I replied, wiping my forehead. I was sweating. "There is nobody I want to save for the rest of my life than you, and nobody else I would want to save me. We always talked about a quiet life, and maybe that will never be us, but whatever happens, I want to go through it with you." I dropped to my knee and pulled out the dragon fire ring. "Rose Briar. Will you marry me?"

She chuckled. "You already asked me that, silly, and I said yes."

"I know," I replied. "But the last time was in the middle of a right shit situation, and I don't want that to be the way I remember what's supposed to be one of the happiest moments of our lives. So, will you?"

"You're silly." A smile crept across her face before she leapt from the bed into my arms. "Yes, yes, yes. Of course I will!"

We fell to the ground, kissing until we were breathless, and when she pulled away finally, I slid the dragon fire ring onto her finger. "That makes me the happiest person in the whole world. No, the whole universe."

"Me too." She smiled as she looked at the new ring. "But...why did you get me a new ring?"

"This is a very special ring," I said. "Rama gave it to me, along with this necklace. We can use these to reach other across the cosmos—"

"Yeah, that's all fine and good," Rose interrupted. "But I really love the one you gave me."

"This is one of the rarest objects in the universe. Nothing I could ever buy you is as beautiful as this dragon fire ring."

"Sure," she said slowly. "But that other one, you bought it for me—it even has an inscription! I love it because it was special to you."

I handed her the diamond ring. "You're weird, but here you go."

She pulled Rama's ring off her finger and replaced it with my ring. Then, she slid the dragon fire ring onto her middle finger. "My gods this is gaudy. I much prefer yours."

"It's so small. It's all I could afford."

She shook her head. "I thought it was perfect, but I guess this one is nice, too."

She met my lips, and when they connected, a spark rippled through my body as she gave herself to me, fully, completely, utterly, and I did the same for her. We might never see each other again after Rama had his way with us, but while we were together, we would make every moment count.

CHAPTER 26

ARIEL

Vivian led me deep into the darkness of Nox's cavern, far past where I was comfortable. When we reached a fork in the path, instead of going left or right she dove deep down into a barely perceptible crevice. The crack tightened as we went along, until I was sure her goal was to bind me in the hole and make me her prisoner, but just as it narrowed to a point where I could barely use my arms, we broke through to an enormous cave opening, with brilliant white light streaking down from the sky and focusing on a spot on the ground.

She made her way up to the top of the cavern, and we poked our heads out of the water. Nox had built a living space there, complete with furniture, and behind it all, carved into the craggily rock, stood an enormous vault.

"See, I told you," Vivian said. "I'll bet you thought I was going to murder you or something."

I nodded. "I did at that."

"And you still kept following me. I severely underestimated you. You must have the resolve of stone."

I pressed my hands on the edge of the cold stone and

pulled myself up. "I have to admit, that compliment almost makes this all worth it. I am confused about something, though. How did you find this place?"

"Nox showed me," Vivian replied. "She was a lonely woman, and I provided her a certain...companionship over the many years of her solitude."

I stared at her, but she avoided my gaze. "You don't have anything to be ashamed about with me. You liked her, and she must have liked you enough to bring you here."

"I liked to watch her work, poring over notes and muttering for hours. Every now and again she'd glance in my direction and smile."

"And in all that time she never talked to you about the eye of Rapunzel?"

"She never talked to me about anything she kept in her vault, or about her work at all. Eventually, I stopped asking." Vivian shook her head. "If it's as dangerous as you claim, then I'm glad she didn't. Mostly, we would talk nonsense, or, well, you know, not talk at all."

I stood, wringing my clothes dry. "*Siccum.*"

The rest of the wetness leached from my clothes and onto the ground around me. Vivian raised her eyebrows approvingly. "That's a nice trick."

She hopped up on the rock and muttered to herself, pressing her left hand against her fin and her right against her throat. When she was done, her hands glowed a deep magenta, and she let out a small yelp as her fin turned into two legs, covered in scales. The gills on the side of her neck closed up, and she took a deep gasp of air.

"So is that," I replied. "What would your mother think?"

"Queen Ursula isn't my mother any more than you are

my sister, but you're right, she would hate it. You know how she feels about the surface. Please don't tell her."

"I won't," I replied. "But you seem to have a deep hatred for the surface, too. Why would you want legs?"

She chuckled. "It's very hard to sleep in a bed, or even get to one, without them. Help me up."

I took her outstretched arms and pulled her to her feet. There was softness in her face I had never seen before, as if this place brought out a calmness that she could never show anywhere else. "This cave suits you."

Her wet feet slapped on the ground. "It's the only place I feel...safe. I know Ursula has kept you out of the politics of royal life. Basically, it's hard to know who to trust, so you must always be on your guard. Nox and Ursula are the only two people more powerful than me in the whole ocean, and while my mother expected much of me, Nox asked for nothing except my company. It was nice to be with some-body who didn't care that I was the heir to the Forgotten Sea."

"That does sound nice. I never knew that about you."

She looked over at me, and her jagged teeth formed into a smile. "It's probably why I hate you so much. You are so blissfully unaware of it all, wearing your ignorance like a badge of honor." That stung. She stopped when she saw my face. "I'm sorry if that offends you, but it is true. I have learned better than to hold my tongue over the years, espe-cially with those below my position."

"Rude," I said. "Even if it's true."

"I don't care."

Nox's bed, curio, vanity, and other bedroom essentials were cubbied away in a rock enclosure on one side of the vault, with several couches and tables on the other, arranged for company. It didn't look like she ever used them to entertain.

"I don't suppose you know the combination, do you?" I asked.

"She liked me well enough, but not that well."

I stroked my chin. "She doesn't seem like the kind of person who would keep the combination to such a thing laying around..."

A sly smile crept across Vivian's face. "She might not have liked me enough to give it to me, that doesn't mean I haven't been able to discern it on my own." She placed her right hand on the vault and muttered some commands. "Come help me with this."

I placed my hand next to hers. "What do I do?"

"Place your left hand on the vault and grab my hand with your right. This is a powerful spell and needs the both of us to wield it." She held out her hand. "Don't worry. It won't hurt."

A sudden shock of heat rushed through me when I took her hand and she continued the incantation. The large metal wheel that held the massive door closed spun furiously, then stopped with a click and turned the other way. It did this several times before finally the wheel stopped spinning and the door cracked open. A century's worth of air leaked out at once.

"Now, let's go find your precious eye."

CHELLE

After we'd celebrated our engagement properly, Rose and I fell back into bed and stared up at the ceiling, wrapping ourselves tightly around each other as we caught our breath.

"The closer we get to leaving, the more I think this is a bad idea," Rose said, pulling me tightly to her.

"That's where you and I differ," I said. There was a look of hope in her eye, as if I was about to offer encouragement. "I always thought this was a bad idea."

There was a knock on the door, and Maricel pushed it open without waiting for a response. "I'm sorry for the interruption. I waited until I no longer heard..." She stepped forward timidly, holding an armful of clothes, her eyes on the ground. "Mister Rama wishes to inform you that it's time, and you are to meet him in the library presently. I have taken the liberty to find clothes fitting your destination, Miss Rose." She held them up. "I'll leave them here for you."

She bowed and left the clothes on the vanity. Once the

door had closed again, Rose burst out laughing. "Oh my god, why did that feel like being busted by my mother?"

"It was definitely nothing like that." I poked her in the ribs. "Your mother would have run me out of the house with a shotgun."

"She totally would have." Rose laughed again, then looked at the pile of clothes. "Do you think I have time for a shower?"

"Probably not, but I think you should take it anyway." I rolled out of bed and hopped onto the cold marble floor. "I don't know when I'm going to get a chance to see you again, if ever, so I'm perfectly happy to keep your stink on me."

"That's disgusting," Rose replied, sticking out her tongue.

"I think it's kind of romantic."

"You would."

She didn't respond because she was looking at a note on top of the clothes. She handed it to me. It was written in Rama's handwriting: *No, you don't have time for a shower. Yes, when I say presently, I mean right now. Maricel took a stab at your measurements. She's very good, but if something needs to be exchanged, then now is the time.*

P.S. – No, I would change my mind about the clothes, and there will be no substitutions.

P.P.S – These are Rose's clothes, Chelle. Yours have been hung in the closet.

Maricel brought Rose some black jeans, paired with a black T-shirt with a white circle spray-painted on it. Between the shirt and pants were a collection of accessories, including a watch, hair tie, and a pair of brass knuckles. There was nothing special about them, and I wondered how they'd been selected.

"Oh good. I was sick of wearing this dress," Rose said with a shrug. She always had such a good demeanor about everything and took everything in stride. She held up the T-shirt. "Good thing I don't have dandruff, huh?"

"Very," I replied. "Though something tells me that there's a spell for that, even though I never trafficked in anything so vain."

She shook her hair out. "Luckily, I don't have to worry about it. My hair has always been perfect. The one thing about me I actually like."

I brushed my hand over her cheek. "You're perfect."

She kissed me again, softly and sweetly, before turning to the closet. "What do you think he brought for you?"

"Something terrible, I'm sure." In the closet was a blue sequin dress with a deep slit up the side, like I was a cocktail singer straight out of the 1950s. "Yup, that's terrible all right."

Rose doubled over laughing. "Oh my god. I love this so much. I can't wait to see this."

"I'm not wearing that."

"OOOH!" she said, taking back the note. "There's something on the back."

She turned the note over and I read over her shoulder: *Yes, you are.*

"I'm going to kill him," I said, crumpling the paper.

"Let's save the universe and free Gabrielle, first. Then, depending on how we feel, we can kill him."

"Easy for you to say. You have a cute outfit. I have to wear this."

"I absolutely cannot wait for you to change."

I held the dress up to myself. I never wore dresses, even at Rose's coronation, and especially not tight ones that restricted my movement. I unzipped the back and slipped it on, wriggling for every inch.

"Zip me up," I said with a deep resignation.

Rose slid the zipper up my back and attached the clasp at the top. "All done."

I spun around toward her, the bottom of my dress catching in the wind. "How do I look?"

Rose stared, taking me in. "So wonderful. If we survive this, we're totally going to the opera."

"If we survive this, I'm never wearing a dress again." I pulled at the fabric, trying to get it to stop pinching my stomach. "I hate this so much."

"Well, then I have something that might make you feel better. I know you always like me grungy, despite the fact I absolutely hate it."

I watched Rose change into her outfit. She found some black lipstick and eyeliner in the vanity. When she finally topped her hair with the skull beanie, she looked like one of the Goth goddesses I'd fallen in love with all too often in high school.

"How do I look?"

"So hot, babe." I pulled her close to me. "If we didn't have to be somewhere..."

"But you do!" a voice shouted through the door. "Get downstairs!"

Rose held up her hand. "Wait, I have an idea." She pulled the dragon fire ring off her finger and held it up to her face. "*Fingunt.*"

"What are you doing?"

The gold around the gem molded from a complete circle into an unconnected one. She pressed it to her nose and muttered something under her breath. When she looked up, it was attached through her septum in a bull ring, making her all the hotter.

"Better?"

"So, so, so much better." I pointed to her engagement ring. "What about that, though? I have a feeling you won't want to tell people you're engaged wherever you're going."

"Well, I'm not taking it off, either." She held it tight as she brought her mouth down to it. "*Evanescet.*" The ring glittered for a moment before disappearing into the ether. She spent a minute touching her finger. "Good, I still feel it. Just have to remember not to catch it on something."

"You can take it off. I don—"

"No!" Rose clasped her hand over her finger. "I'm never taking it off again. No matter what."

I held out my arm. "Come here."

We kissed again, and again. It was all I could do not to bring her back to the bed. I controlled myself, barely, as I held her close, not wanting to let her go. All I wanted to do was look into her eyes and get lost in our love for one more moment. But the future of the universe was at stake, and for some reason, it was up to us to save the day yet again. How had we ever agreed to something so foolish?

Probably because we were idiots.

CHAPTER 28

NIMUE

I still didn't believe Cassandra, at least not the part where she told me she was still on my side, but she might have been right about being able to turn the princesses against Hastur. Delilah seemed amenable to the possibility, and if the others were even a fraction as wounded as she was, mentally if not physically, then they should relish the opportunity to take down their abuser. It was only a simple matter of lining up the dominos and proving that I was the right person to put their trust in, when everyone else they'd trusted had let them down.

When I peeked out of my room again, Elvira had left her post, perhaps convinced that I was no longer going to run, or willing to let me do so if I chose to act foolhardy. She had delivered her warning, and it was a compelling one, but that was not the reason I chose to stay. I chose to stay because nobody should be forced to live in a nightmare. I worked my whole life to break myself free of horrible men and make sure they got their comeuppance. There was nothing but warped malice in the King in Yellow's amber eyes; he needed to be stopped. This went far beyond my deal with Baba, and down into the depths of my soul. His injustice would not stand while I drew breath.

I took a swig of the black medicine and crept down the hall. The corridors of the castle curved endlessly, and it wasn't long before I had no idea how to find my way back to my room. The walls and doors all looked the same, save for the slight differences in the monsters carved into them. Somewhere I heard the crack of a whip and woman's whimpering, and I was confident that the sound would lead me to Hastur's chambers, and whatever torture he had summoned Delilah to bear.

After what felt like hours, I found myself standing outside of the room where the whimpers rang out like wails. There were two doors, each carved with heinous acts and framed with another etching of haggard faces. As I moved, they seemed to move with me, crying for relief that I could not give.

I had seen my share of torture. You had no choice as queen. Some lips only loosened after lashings. Eventually I grew numb to it, though it never pleased me. It is not an easy thing to inflict pain on someone, but it was clear Hastur reveled in it. If my suspicions were right, then he fed off that suffering, literally using it to sustain himself. If that was his strength, then I would find a way to exploit it. But first, I had to bring the princesses to my side.

I stood outside of Hastur's chambers until my feet throbbed, listening to Delilah screaming, but after many hours, the cracking and wailing stopped, replaced by grunting and panting. I shivered at the thought of Hastur touching her skin, caressing it, violating it a second time. When he was done, the door opened and Delilah fell onto the ground, sweaty and shivering at the same time. Blood streamed down her white dress, which had been replaced hastily and was ripped in places.

I knelt next to her as she trembled. "Are you okay?"

She looked at me, and the powerful eyes I had seen not long ago were haunted by a wounded brokenness. The green glow that made her so striking was gone.

"Just leave me," she said, tears streaming down her face. "We are to be alone with our thoughts when he is finished with us."

She tried to stand, but her knees knocked together, and she only stayed upright because I lurched forward and grabbed her. "Come now. Nobody should have to be alone after all that."

We walked slowly and stopped often. I passed Elvira in the hall, and she turned away from us, but not before a curt nod, approving my kindness. Even though the hallways were a maze, the statues were all distinct pieces of horror, and I used my memory of them to reconstruct my way back to my room, helped along by Delilah's muted cries when I couldn't find the way.

I pushed open the door and laid her face down on the bed. She protested, muttering about going back to her room to be alone, but she was too weak to fight, and when I went to find some water, she grabbed my hand so that I could not leave her side.

Together, the princesses would be a formidable force. No wonder Hastur didn't want them to be around each other, especially at their most vulnerable.

It had always been this way...but not anymore.

CHAPTER 29

ROSE

I had never seen Chelle as beautiful as she was in that evening gown, but it was something I could never tell her. She absolutely hated it, though not as much as the silver stiletto shoes she found waiting for her on the closet floor.

"I'm not wearing these," she grumbled, but there was resignation in her voice.

"Before we get downstairs," I said. "There's something that I need to tell you."

She glanced up at me while fiddling with the shoe strap. "And you waited until now."

"Well, I was asleep, and then you proposed, and then we were...busy," I said. "But the last time I fell asleep I dreamed of Urgu."

"Without pills?"

"Somehow. Maybe it was Hypnos's magic that brought me there." I frowned. "He summoned me to tell me not to trust Rama."

"Well, that's obvious." Chelle took my hand and we descended the stairs. "I knew I liked that god for some reason."

"Don't give him too much credit. Remember, his disappearance is what got us messed up with the gods in the first place."

"Oh...right." Chelle wobbled onto the landing. "Yeah, I knew there was a reason I hated him."

"Look at you," Rama said, coming out of the library. "A vision in blue, and a...something in black."

"Hey!" I shot back. "I look hot, and nothing you can say will make me think otherwise."

"You are very hot, babe." Chelle touched my cheek. "The nose ring is a really nice touch."

"Not my type," Rama said. "I prefer a girl with some class."

Chelle shot him a look and said, "With a stick up her ass, you mean."

Rama grinned. "That wholly depends on how the night goes."

"Gross," I said. "Ew, ew, ew."

"Please," Rama said. "You two were loud enough to shake the whole house. Let's not pretend like you're a prude."

"I didn't say I was a prude. I said that was gross, and I stick by it, no pun intended."

"Let's just get started, shall we?" Rama rubbed his hands together and met us at the bottom of the stairs. "The jobs I have for you couldn't be more different, and frankly, I would much prefer it if you swapped places. After all, one of you was a queen, and the other nearly stopped Queen Zabasha single handedly, but we're running out of time, and I have to work with what I have."

"You're starting to scare me," Chelle said. "And I don't scare easily."

"You should be scared," Rama said. "That is a good instinct."

"Ugh." I rolled my eyes. "We get it. Meeting Odin will be dangerous, even if Chelle will look fabulous doing it. What will I be doing while she's in her pageant, and why do I look like Goth Barbie?"

"You are going to retrieve something for me."

"What?" Chelle said. "A coupon to Hot Topic?"

"I don't know what that is, but I know I'm not sending you for something as plebeian as a coupon. This is one of the more powerful objects in the universe...my Brahmastra. The weapon I once used to fell great beasts and gods alike to earn my place in the Heavens."

"And how will this help save the universe?" I asked. "Are we just going to stab the Board to death? That sounds a little too straightforward for you."

"Nothing so gauche." He cleared his throat. "While we don't know Nox's plan, we know enough parts of it to make some guesses. One of them is that she is trying to open the pathway to the Dark Planet and bring Rapunzel back into the world."

"Rapunzel?" Chelle chuckled. "Really?"

"Yes, really. She is the most powerful witch in the universe, and the only human who has bypassed the gods and attained their power without permission. We don't know exactly what Nox is planning, but we know that it involves Rapunzel, which means we need a key to unlock the door, and unfortunately, that key has been lost."

"So why aren't we going looking for the key?" I asked.

Rama shook his head. "Because that would be like finding a needle in a haystack. We're going to forge a new one, and in order to do that, we need the same metal it was forged from."

"From your weapon," I said slowly. "You need to melt it down to make the key."

He nodded. "There are only five others in the universe that know this besides the two of you. If you tell anybody, it will be the end of us."

"Is one of those people Aditi?" I asked, remembering that she was fighting against Athena to give us time to escape.

He nodded. "As are Hepit and iNyanga, which is why we need to move fast. It is only a matter of time before they break, or Zeus finds some other way to make them speak."

"Then what are we standing around here for?" Chelle said. "This dress is riding up in all the wrong places. Let's get on with it."

"Are you ready?" Rama asked me.

"Absolutely not."

"It will be fine. We think we have tracked the location of the Brahmastra to a planet on the outer rim. It is being guarded by Kadlu, a vicious and powerful god who would love nothing more than to eviscerate me with my own weapon. She loves new blood and power. Once she finds out you have magic, her attention will turn to you." He walked across the room to a small, wooden chest laying on top of a small cabinet. "When you show her where to find this, she will have no choice but to let you into her graces."

"What is it?" I asked.

"The Circle of Trust is not the only organization working to bring down the Board, just the most well-funded and the most thoughtful. Kadlu is more militant. She's looking for a way to kill a god." He opened the chest and pulled out a golden dagger I recognized from Red's arsenal. "This is one of the few objects that can do it, and your friend happened to have it on her when she was captured. Whatever you do, do not tell Kadlu you got it from me. Lie if you have to."

There it was, lying. The exact thing Hypnos warned me about not doing to Kadlu. Rama promised not to harm Chelle, but he made no such promise to me. Was he trying to put me in danger? Was that part of his plan, or just an incidental benefit of it?

"Are you sure Rose can handle this?" Chelle asked, casting a quick glance in my direction. "I have to admit, as much as I love Rose, she's not much of a field operative."

I wheeled on her. "Hey, I kept my cool at high tea with dignitaries and pretended their stories weren't boring. I can literally lie my way into anything at this point."

Rama pressed the piece of paper into my hand. "Exchange this information for the location of the Brahmastra. She will ask you to help steal it for her, but do not agree. It is a suicide mission."

"I won't let you down."

"It's not me you should worry about. If any of us should fail, the whole universe will be let down."

"No pressure, though," Chelle said. She flashed a brilliant smile but her voice shook. "We'll both do great."

I took her hands in mine. "I love you."

"I love you, too. Don't die."

"You either."

CHAPTER 30

RED

I knew somebody dastardly would come for me sooner or later, and the worst part was knowing there was nothing I could do about it. They would take me where they wanted, when they wanted. I prided myself on being independent; on doing whatever I wanted to do when I wanted to do it. I had never been caged so long in my long life.

Yes, I had been imprisoned before, naturally, but there was always a way out, and within hours, or at the most, days, I would be free once again. There was no escaping the Crystal Keep. Every rock face was smooth, and even if I found a way out, the guards were nearly indestructible crystal golems. Even if I somehow could defeat their indominable bodies, it would take more than that to get past Athena, who seemed to have it in for me.

I stared down at my hands, willing them to show me a way out of this impossible situation, and then I heard the sound of metal tapping. Was Athena coming for me again? The steps sounded lighter than hers, which shook the ground. These steps sounded like they halfway floated on the air. A shadow hid the strip of light under my door, which creaked open to reveal a woman wearing a red sari and metal-tipped flat shoes. With her soft features and chains that hung across her head and face, she looked nothing like a soldier. The tray in her hands had a sandwich and a glass of milk on it.

"Hello, Gabrielle. May I come in?"

"It's your prison," I replied. "I don't think I have much choice in the matter."

"Still, I would like your permission. I am not a guard, and I have no stake in your continued oppression, I assure you. I have brought you some food from a friend who knows how terrible the food is in this place."

I slid to the back of the cell. "Be my guest."

She bowed and placed the tray down in front of me, then sat on the bed. "They have told me that I would die if I saw you, considering how lethal you are with your hands."

"I'm a fighter, sure, but I don't like killing."

"Most who don't like killing simply don't kill. That is not the case with you, is it?" She must have seen me looking at the food, because she gestured to it. "For instance, I do not like killing, and thus, I have never killed. Not once, in my whole life."

"Good for you."

There was a long silence, and she held out her hand to the tray. "Please, it is not much, but eat."

I grabbed the sandwich without another word and took a big bite. Peanut butter and jelly, and the milk washed it down perfectly. "Why are you here?"

My words were bitter, but she didn't appear to take them personally, responding to my spite with a sweet smile. "I am here on behalf of a benefactor who has a vested interest in your survival."

"Even Zeus seems to want me alive, so that is not saying much."

She nodded. "You're right. He has his own ends in mind, but we do not approve of them. Perhaps I should be more precise. My benefactor has a vested interest in your freedom."

I took another huge bite and muttered around it. "They must be very powerful to get you into this place."

"You might say that. He would very much like to help you escape this burden, but before he does, he has a question."

"Of course he does. Powerful men usually do. What is it then?"

"What would you do for your freedom?"

I stopped eating and placed the sandwich down. "There it is."

"What?"

"Usually when somebody comes to extort my services, they have a set of terms already, and they do better than a peanut butter and jelly sandwich."

She cocked her head. "Was it not to your liking? I can bring something else next time."

"Steak and potatoes with wine, if you're going to ask me to kill someone."

She took a pen and notepad out of the thin air and wrote a note to herself. "Noted. Now, what makes you think we're going to ask you to kill somebody?"

"Context clues. The way you probed to see how I really felt about killing. When you've been doing this for as long as me, you get very good at reading the clues. So, who am I supposed to kill?"

She held up her hand. "It is impolite to speak of such things here. I was simply sent to gauge your interest in meeting my benefactor and bring him a report of your condition."

"My condition?"

"How you look, sound, feel. Whether you are gaunt and pale or healthy and strong."

She eyed me up and down, taking in everything from my hair down to my toes. I hadn't been stared at that way by somebody that wasn't looking to kill me or screw me in a long time. Simply having somebody look at me as if I were a human, after days of being treated like I was unworthy of life, filled me with all sorts of emotions ranging from relief to anger to gratitude.

"And what will you tell him?" I finally managed to say.

"Again, that depends on whether you want to meet him or not. I could just as easily tell him you are pathetic and feeble, if you would rather stay in this place."

I stiffened. "No, please. That is the last thing I want."

"Then answer my question. What would you do to be free of this place?"

"Anything, except hurt my friends."

"Very good." She stood, brushing herself off from whatever might have been lurking on my prison bed. "I'm afraid I need to bring the tray with me. In your hands, they could be lethal."

"In my hands, anything is lethal," I replied, staring at her for a long moment before wolfing down the rest of the sandwich and milk. "Do you know I used to be lactose intolerant before I arrived in Urgu? Though that's not what we called it, back when I was alive."

"I didn't know that, but it is quite a boring story," she replied, picking up the tray. "I hope you have better anecdotes for my benefactor."

"I'll make a note of it."

"Please do." The woman walked out of the room, locking the door and vanishing as if she never existed in the first place. Somehow, her kindness made me feel the loneliness even deeper, and I hated her for making my heart feel as heavy as the darkness weighing down upon it. But it wasn't long before I drifted off to sleep, my belly full for the first time in days.

CHAPTER 31

ROSE

I was not a field operative by any stretch of the imagination. Chelle was right about that, even if it hurt to hear her say it. I had never been "on assignment," and my unique set of skills did not include stealth, like Red, or brute strength, like Chelle.

"I'm not sure about this," I told Rama as he hung Patrisiol on the front door of his mansion.

"Nonsense," he assured me. "If you can save a realm, you can handle this little mission."

"I'm not sure they are the same, and I'm not good at subterfuge."

"Weren't you a queen?" Patrisiol asked as Rama adjusted her so that she was straight on the door.

"For like, five seconds," I replied.

"Don't sell yourself short," Chelle added. "You were in training for like, a month before the coronation."

"Yeah, and Queen Aine could barely keep me from putting my foot in my mouth every day."

Rama stopped futzing with Patrisiol and turned to me.

"I appreciate your concern, but Red is in prison, Nox is captured, your paramour is needed for other, more pressing business, Aditi has been locked up along with both Hepit and iNyanga, and I am desperately trying to keep our fragile alliance from falling apart now that we have been seeing increased pressure from the Board."

We were quiet, absorbing all of Rama's information. Finally, I shook my head and said, "There has to be somebody else."

"There isn't," Rama bit at me before recomposing himself. "You are not my first, second, or tenth choice, either, but given the circumstances, I am stuck throwing a porcelain doll into a demolition derby and bringing a bull to a china shop."

Chelle grabbed my arms. "It's going to be okay. Just, don't smile, okay?"

I caught myself smiling and curled the sides of my lips back down. "I can do that."

"I know you can." Chelle kissed my cheek. "You're gonna do great."

"Are you saying that because you believe it, or just to calm my nerves?"

"Both," she replied, but even then, I wasn't sure if she was telling the truth. It didn't much matter, though. Unless I wanted to run away, which I was sure was what Chelle wanted, I needed to go where I was needed, and apparently, I was about to become a super spy. She kissed me again and said, "Just remember to breathe. If your hands shake, people will know you're lying."

"But my hands always shake," I replied. "And what happens if my blood sugar gets low? What if I need insulin or something?"

"That won't be a problem," Rama said. "I've taken care of that."

I turned to him. "What do you mean, you 'fixed' that?"

"I mean that I noticed you had a chemical imbalance and fixed it for you. I'm surprised that none of the other gods had done it, honestly."

"You fixed me? I wasn't broken, jerk." I stomped toward him. "You had no right to do anything without my permission. Touching me without my consent is such a violation."

He blinked a few times. "I was just trying to help. Would you like me to change you back? It wouldn't be any trouble for me."

"That's not the—" I growled at him. "No, I don't want to go back to how it was, but I didn't want to be fixed, either. None of the other gods I've met cured me because I didn't ask, and they aren't vio—" I took a moment to breathe. "Thank you, I guess."

I wasn't thankful that he took it upon himself to change my body without asking, but now I knew that was the type of god he was. Even the most selfish of them didn't violate me in such a blatant manner and then expect me to thank him for the privilege. Now, I was even more wary of him than I had been after my meeting with Hypnos.

Rama scratched his eyebrow. "I'll never understand you humans."

"All we want is to be allowed to live a healthy, peaceful —you know what? We don't have time for this. I can't look at you right now. Just let me go and do whatever I have to do."

"As you wish." He opened the door and a white light plumed in. "It took everything we had to track down Kadlu, and even then, we're only about fifty-fifty we found even a hint of her. I don't have to tell you how important is it that you track down this weapon, right?"

"No," I replied. "I got it. Go have your fun."

"You think this is going to be fun?" Chelle said with a light chuckle. "Trust me, there is nothing fun about wearing this get-up and having to schmooze with crusty old gods. I would do just about anything to trade places with you."

"Same," I said. "Your mission actually sounds quite lovely."

"You're so weird."

"I'm weird?" I replied. "You want to go slumming with criminals. I want to have a fancy dinner and drink delicious wine. How am I the weird one?"

"Girls, girls," Rama said. "You're both weird. All humans are." He gestured to the door. "Now, if you don't mind. We are all out of 'cute banter' time, so quit stalling."

"Fine," I said before a long sigh and a longer silence. "I'm just scared."

Chelle grabbed my hands tenderly. "You should be."

I scoffed. "Thanks."

"Not helping," Rama added.

"I'm saying this stuff is scary and you should be scared when you're doing something scary, but it shouldn't stop you. Remember," she said, placing a hand on my chest, "if worse comes to worst, you have the power of two gods coursing through you. You can mess some stuff up."

"But please don't," Rama interjected again. "It would absolutely blow your cover, and seriously hamper our ability to get my weapon back."

"I'll use it as a last resort," I said, looking down at my hands. "But it is nice to know that I have them if I need them."

"But don't need them," Rama squeezed in at the end of my words. "And now, off you go."

My stomach tightened when I let go of Chelle's hands. I collected myself, then walked through the white light into the great unknown. *You can do this, Rose. Even if you don't believe it, just keep saying it, and maybe some of Chelle's confidence will rub off on you.*

CHAPTER 32

ARIEL

Vivian pulled on the vault door to open it. "Help me."

I grabbed onto the edge of the door and pulled, but it wasn't budging for either of us. "I have a better idea."

I cast a spell to yank it open. An orange, spindly arm shot from my chest and latched onto the door. Together with Vivian, the arm worked to wrestle it open. It was clearly made for a god, and we were little more than two mortals, powerful perhaps, but nothing compared to a god.

By the time we were able to squeeze inside, the two of us were exhausted, panting for air and using the craggily rock wall to hold us up.

"What do you think is inside?" I asked, still recovering my breath.

"I've been wondering that for years, but every time I asked, Nox deflected. I am excited to find out, and that's an emotion I don't feel often."

I brushed off my hands. "Then what are we waiting for?"

I slid past her inside the vault and couldn't believe my eyes. We were like ants in a labyrinth. Shelves, stacked hundreds of feet high, continued until they disappeared into the white light cast across the room.

"This place is massive," I said. "We'll never find anything in here."

We traveled down the pristine white corridors, searching for the something that could be construed as a map or ledger. After nearly an hour, it didn't look like we had moved very far, with the vault door still looming large behind us.

"This is going to take forever," I said. "And that's assuming that something like a map even exists. It might be in some sort of pocket dimension, or in a glass vial around her neck, or something like that."

"That's it!" Vivian shouted, pulling me back toward the door. "You're a genius."

"I don't see how. I didn't do anything special."

"Of course you didn't, but you jogged my memory. Often, when I came to see Nox, she was writing in a large book. One night I asked her what she was working on. She obfuscated, but I was able to see her writing. I'm pretty sure it was a ledger, or some sort of list."

"That's great!" I hurried along beside her. "Maybe it can tell us what's inside this vault."

"Well, it's great and it isn't. The good news is that she did keep it in a pocket dimension or something, because whenever I came, she muttered something to herself and slid it away into the ether, but I know exactly where she hid it."

"Let me guess the bad part. You don't know the spell."

"Correct," Vivian replied. "But you could go into my memories and find the spell, couldn't you? I mean, you said you had the blessing of Hypnos."

"I mean, you're already technically dreaming, right? I'm not sure I can make you dream again."

"Sure you can. Nox led me through my memories a bunch of times. I can teach you the spells and—"

"I don't want to mess with your mind. It's too dangerous." I looked down at my hands. "And I'm not powerful enough. There must be some other way."

"There isn't." Her voice was stern. "Don't be a baby. Hypnos controls everything about this place, and he gave his power to you. I know you can do it." Vivian looked at me doe-eyed and helpless. "Please, Ariel, you have to try."

My lips pursed at her wounded expression. "Why are you so interested in helping me? What's your angle?"

"No angle. I just want to help."

I stopped dead in my tracks. "That doesn't sound like you at all, sis. Don't lie to me. You clearly want something. Before we got here, you were trying to kill me, and then suddenly, once I saved you it was like a candle flickered on and you became exceedingly helpful." I got in her face. "What are you after? Tell me, or I will leave this vault and lock it for good."

Vivian huffed. "Fine. Do you know about the Trident of Atlantis?"

"Of course, it was the symbol of royalty in the seas for centuries before it was lost to time."

"Not time," Vivian said. "That is a convenient lie that slowly morphed into the truth. The truth is that Nox stole the trident from us, and the uneasy alliance we have kept for generations to guard her and protect her came from her possession of the trident. If I take it back, we can use it to claim our rightful rule of not just the Forgotten Sea, but the ocean that surrounds Urgu."

"And were you ever going to tell me about this?"

She pulled a face. "No, of course not. I was planning on finding the trident and locking you inside forever. This place has a magical barrier on it, so you wouldn't be able to use your powers to escape."

"You admit that to me freely and still expect me to help you?"

"Yes, because you are a naturally good person and because you want something, too, and the only way we'll get it is together."

I held out my hand. "Swear you will not betray me."

"A magical binding, sis? Isn't that a little old school? Remember, you can't cast spells in here."

I shook my head. "Not a magical binding, just your word as a royal that you will not betray me. In return, I will help you. Look me in the eyes and tell me you won't lock me in here."

She didn't hesitate. She grabbed my arm and looked deep into my eyes. "I swear that I am not deceiving you."

"On your honor as a mermaid and heir to Ursula's throne?"

"On my honor, and that of my whole house. Is that good enough?"

It wasn't, but she was right. I needed her to get the ledger, and that meant trusting her, even if it went against my greatest instincts. I would need to watch myself around her, because I believed her as far as I could throw her, and that wasn't far.

CHAPTER 33

CHELLE

"This is where I leave you," Rama said, after closing the door to Rose's destiny and opening it again to mine.

"What do you mean, this is where you leave me?" I threw out my hands. "I thought you were presenting me to Odin. How can you present me if you aren't even there?"

"I'm sorry, but something came up that can't be controlled, as is the way with these types of things. Just remember to keep your chin up and shoulders back. It really accentuates your chest. Odin is a chest man."

"I hate you so much," I growled. "So, you're just feeding me to the wolves, then, and expect me to figure it all out on my own without your help?"

He held a finger in the air. "What I must do concerns your friend Gabrielle, and the stability of the entire Circle. Are you telling me you can't present yourself to Odin and not embarrass yourself?"

"Yes, that is exactly what I'm saying."

"You can fight off gods, and save a kingdom, but you can't stop from tripping over your tongue?"

"No, I can't. How many times do I have to say it? I was

planning on just shutting my mouth and nodding politely while you talked."

He pulled me back to the door. "That is a good instinct. Say as little as possible. The more you say, the more Frigg will have to use against you."

"Frigg?"

"Odin's wife, and keeper of his house. She only responds to the possibility of power." Rama looked down. "Where are your shoes?"

"I didn't want to wear them."

Rama snapped his fingers and the silver stiletto shoes appeared on my feet. "You don't have a choice."

He moved aside so I could clatter past him. As I went by, failing miserably to find my balance, he slapped me on the ass and said something about having a good time. I didn't have time to respond before I fell into the white light and the door closed.

I landed on the floor in a crumpled pile and grabbed onto a table to pull myself up, more than a little awkwardly. The table was unstable, and it collapsed, sending a ceremonial vase crashing to the ground. The sound of it echoed through the hallways.

I squeezed my eyes shut. This was exactly what I was worried about this whole time: I hadn't been here for more than a few seconds and I already made a fool of myself. Not a banner day for me.

I touched the dragon fire necklace. I wanted so badly to call out to Rose, but when I looked down at it the murky red and orange cleared, and I saw through the other ring that she was on the move. I didn't want her worrying about me. She had her own mission to complete.

"Oh, my word," a breathy, excitable voice tittered. "Are you all right?"

Heels clamped on the floor, and I craned my neck to see an older woman with gray and white streaked hair. She wore a long blue dress, much like mine without the sequins, accented by golden ropes and a fringed low collar.

"I think so," I replied, taking her outstretched hand. "My pride hurts more than anything."

"Well, there is no shame in this house, girl." She eyed the broken vase. "Oh, bother."

I stared at the floor. "I'm so sorry about that. It looks really expensive. I guess I hurt that as well."

She smiled sweetly. "It's okay, dear. That's one of the benefits of being a god."

She spun her finger counterclockwise, and the vase reformed itself, rewinding until it sat on the end table as it had before.

"Pretty impressive."

"It's not really anything," she said. "My husband is quite clumsy, and it's handy in a pinch when he stumbles all over the house like a drunken mule."

I stifled a laugh. "Does that mean you are Frigg, then?"

She smiled. "I am. And you must be Michelle."

"Chelle is fine," I replied. "But yes, I am."

She eyed me up and down. "Let me guess, Rama demanded you wear that to see me, right? It doesn't look like your style."

"I—" I didn't know how to act, but I certainly didn't want to lie to a goddess. That seemed like a big no-no. The only advice Rama gave me was not to say much. "He thought it would be appropriate."

"One of the great joys of my husband not being a member of that accursed Board is that we don't have to entertain, which means we can dress as we like."

"You look very nice, ma'am."

"I know, my dear, but that is because it is what makes me comfortable." She looked me over again. "You look like a jeans and T-shirt kind of girl, if you ask me. Tell me, did I nail it?"

"Honestly, ma'am, even if you hadn't, I would tell you yes. But I can say for certain that I am much more comfortable with jeans than this dress."

"Even when I had to dress up for people, I didn't like how constricting they were." She ran her hands along the sides of her waist. "Of course, I loved what they did to my figure. The tradeoffs of beauty and youth."

Frigg was nothing like I expected. I smiled in spite of myself and said, "Yes, ma'am, though I only ever cared if one person thought I was beautiful, and she would've loved me even if I wore a paper sack."

"Well, she sounds very special." She looked up at the snakes on my head. "I love your hair. May I touch it?"

There was nothing I hated more than people asking if they could touch my snakes, but given the situation, and the bumbling entrance I'd made, I didn't feel as though I had much choice. "Of course."

She leaned forward, and they all recoiled. "It's okay, little ones. She's a friend."

"Oh, I hope we can be friends, my dear."

Albie was always my most courageous son, and he slithered forward to accept some scritches. When she was kind to him, the others joined in, and soon all the snakes on my head had joined in to get some pets.

"I neglect them, admittedly," I said. "They do love getting petted."

She doted over them some more and finally said, "Well, come with me. Let us get some food in you. You look like you're wasting away."

I followed her out of the hallway, cautiously optimistic that I couldn't mess it up any more than I already had. Of course, that was wishful thinking. My capacity for messing up polite social interactions was legendary. Meeting people and having them like you was really more Rose's bag. I was more the gruff, feral friend that people accepted because Rose and I were a package deal. It wasn't often because they liked me for me.

CHAPTER 34
NIMUE

Delilah laid face down on my bed for hours, drifting in and out of sleep as I watched over her, cleaning her wounds whenever she was conscious. I hadn't gotten a good sleep since entering the Dark Planet and hadn't had a moment of peace since Hastur flayed off my skin and left it raw to the elements, but I was determined to make sure she was okay before I rested.

Still, I couldn't stop myself from falling into fitful moments of sleep, where I saw the faces of those I'd subjugated flashing past me. The guilt of my rule had eaten at me since being subjected to the Yellow King, and it was getting worse.

Wicked was what they called me, but I truly believed that I was doing what was best—maybe for myself, and not them. What was good for the goose was good for the gander, and parts of the Dream Realm thrived under my rule. I wasn't much worse than the idiot queen Ozma that came before, or any of the kings or queens that ruled over me before I received Hera's blessing.

It wasn't until I decided to put my own needs above the

whole of the kingdom and turned my attention to freeing myself, and by extension the whole of Urgu from their fate as simple souls, that I was seen as wicked. Had I simply carried on the status quo, they might have built statues of me instead of cheering my exile.

"Nnnng." Delilah shifted her weight, and her eyes fluttered open. "Nimue?"

I stroked her silky black hair. "It's me."

She propped herself up with her elbows, wincing. "Why am I here?"

"Don't you remember?"

"No, after the second lashing, everything went mercifully hazy."

I nodded. "Perhaps that is for the best."

Her eyes closed and she let out a pained breath. "It is all coming back to me, but it is still fuzzy."

"After King Ha"—I remembered what Elvira said about not uttering his name—"The King in Yellow was done with you, I helped you back to my room to rest. I tried to heal your wounds, but they would not close, no matter what I did."

"And they won't. Not for a day." She winced again. "The king receives pleasure in pain, lingering or otherwise."

"I have come to realize that," I replied. "It is a horrible fate to be on his wrong side."

"Sometimes, I think he punishes those loyal to him worst of all. He can understand hate, but loyalty is a form of love, which the king finds to be a weakness. He both demands unflinching loyalty and is disgusted by it."

"It must be very hard to put up with him." I looked at her for a long moment. "Do you have a reprieve from his malice for a time?"

"Until he remembers I exist again. For now, he will turn his eyes to others."

"That is good news. At least you have time to recover."

She started to cry, and her tears became sobbing wails. "The worst part is when the pain stops, when you truly believe you might get by without it. It is always in that moment that he strikes again."

"It does sound horrible. I'm so sorry. Have you ever had chocolate?"

"Chocolate?" She sniffled.

"What about ice cream?"

She cocked her head. "Iced...cream?"

"You are in for a treat." I closed my eyes and muttered a simple spell. I hadn't been able to conjure anything since being placed in the dungeons, but my rage at Hastur focused me. A pint of chocolate ice cream appeared in my hand, along with two spoons. "Try it. It's not going to hurt you."

The first step of turning people to your side was providing little kindnesses, showing you are not like the monsters who they've aligned with. The worse the monster, the smaller the consolations necessary. It was easy to show yourself as generous but the victims were often terrified, and it took much more to prove you could protect them from harm. Even then, sometimes it failed to persuade them, and you were stuck with an asset that could not be turned, even after many, many hours spent trying to comfort them.

Delilah was a powerful ally, and if I could get her to turn on the king, then I would have three of the princesses on my side, assuming that Cassandra was not lying. With them, the others would be sure to fall into line soon enough.

"This is really good," Delilah said, licking the spoon clean. "You said this was chocolate ice cream?"

I took a small bite. "That's right. It's a delicacy where I'm from."

"It must be magical there to have something so wondrous. I would like to visit there one day."

I leaned forward and whispered. "I can make that happen for you, Delilah."

She shook her head. "Don't lie to me. We are stuck here forever."

"Hey, I found a way through the gods' veil to get here, didn't I?" I raised my eyebrows and she nodded. "Then what makes you think I couldn't do it again?" She opened her mouth to speak, but nothing came out. "That's okay, dear. Don't worry about giving me an answer. Just enjoy your ice cream. We must enjoy the little things, after all."

She stared down at the ice cream. "The little things are nice."

"Often, they are all we have. And the darker the path, the harder we must cling to these little bits of light." I took another scoop of ice cream. "Trust me, I speak from experience."

"I have no little things like that. I used to have images of my family, but the king took them from me."

"Well," I said, attempting a kind smile, "now you have ice cream."

"Yes. Now I have ice cream."

CHAPTER 35

RED

For days, I waited for another visit from the nice woman who brought me a peanut butter and jelly sandwich, but the only footsteps were the clomping ones of guards, and the clinking golems. I had begun to think that her visit was nothing but an elaborate delusion cooked up by my brain, when the door to my cell opened and she stood in the doorway.

I rubbed my tired eyes. "Is this a dream?"

"Not a dream." She didn't move. I glanced down to see she was now barefoot. "Hurry now."

I leapt from my bed and scurried out of the room. "Thank you for coming for me."

"I'm sorry it took so long. There are many bureaucratic hurdles to overcome in a place like this, but I am glad you never lost faith."

"I wouldn't say that," I replied. "I very much thought you were a delusion until a few seconds ago."

"Who's to say I'm not?" she asked, pulling a granola bar from the sleeve of her sari. "Here, eat this. You'll need your strength for what's to come next."

I salivated, smelling the chocolate chips. It might not have been dignified to stuff the entire thing in my mouth at once, but I didn't care.

The woman smiled. "You're lucky we are not judging you based upon your poise or grace."

I spoke from the sloppy sides of my mouth, still chewing. "Sorry, but—" I choked a bit more down. "I'm just—I haven't had real food since the sandwich you brought me."

"Shhh," she said. "I thought we agreed that was our little secret."

"You're right," I replied. "I'm sorry again. It's just that...I haven't been hungry since I got this body, and now I am constantly ravenous."

"It is the light," she said, pushing open the door to the cell block. "You are solar powered, and without light, you are slowly withering away."

There was no hooting and hollering this time as we passed through the cell block. The prisoners who looked in my direction seemed to stare through me. "So, I'm like a plant."

She chuckled. "We all are, in some way. There are only two truths in this world: light and darkness. We need both to survive, but in balance. You, however, being made of the gods' light, need more of the light than most, which is why we must hurry."

"Hurry before what?" I asked. We pushed through another door and took the stairs down into the depths of the prison corridors below. "It's not like I can die, can I?"

"Your enemies believe so, and if you simply wasted away, then their job would be done, the threat would be neutralized, and they could go about their business as if none of this unpleasantness happened. Of course, there are others of us who are too intrigued by how you were created to allow you to be destroyed so easily."

"And your benefactor is one of those?" I asked.

"He is, but he is not alone, though it might feel that way sometimes."

I was surprised that we were going the same way as Athena had led me to Zeus's chamber. When we rose into the chamber with the statues pointing down at me, my stomach fell to my knees.

"I don't like this, girl. What is your name anyway?"

"That is unimportant. You may call me an apsara, if you must call me anything, as my kind don't often have names."

"Is that your race? Are you an apsara? One of the fairy people?"

"My master has employed us for as long as he can remember. He says we are the only beings he can trust to keep his secrets, and as you know, I take that very seriously."

She pushed open the door to Zeus's hallway, and my heart stopped resting in my stomach and jumped into my throat. "Your benefactor is not Zeus, is it?"

"Of course not." She turned to me when she reached a carved door covered with the depiction of a sun and moon rising simultaneously. "Why would Zeus plot against himself?"

The apsara beckoned me forward. A cold breeze met me, like an air conditioner on a sweltering day. A stained-glass depiction of a kraken provided all the light.

I stepped into the light of the stained glass and instantly began to feel the energy return to my body, and I was filled with a type of strength I had forgotten that I possessed.

"Good, child," a booming voice said from behind the

desk, the speaker hidden by a chair that was turned to the window. "Soak in my light and be reborn in it."

"Lord Brahma," the apsara said, closing the door. "I have returned with your boon."

Brahma stood and clapped his hands once. He had three golden faces situated around a square head, and they spun with his every sentence. "Very good. Were you seen?"

She shook her head. "Only by those who looked up from the shadows, and even then, the minute we passed them, their minds forgot we were there."

"Excellent." Brahma clapped again. "So, you are one of the catalysts that have been causing my brethren so much trouble. Come here, come here. Let me get a look at you."

"I would prefer to stay here, if I may," I replied. "You'll excuse that I don't trust your motives, given that I watched Zeus torture Nox in these very halls."

"Yes, yes. I heard about that. Terrible." He sighed. "Zeus does not speak for this council, despite what he may believe. Some of us have disliked the direction he has taken us for some time but were unable to do anything about it... until now."

"Why now?"

"Because you have arrived." A door, hidden in the wood that lined the room, opened, and a familiar face stepped out.

"Rama?"

He grinned. "It's good to see you again, Red."

CHAPTER 36

CHELLE

Frigg led me through the sinewy hallways of her house. As we walked, she told me that I had entered the mansion through a rarely-used side door, which was why she wasn't there to greet me until she heard the vase shattering. We entered a gigantic kitchen staffed by a half dozen elves and dwarves that scampered around haphazardly cutting vegetables, stirring soup, and grilling meat.

"The elves are phenomenal bakers. They can make a custard to die for. Really anything that takes precision." Frigg said. "But they have no feel for fire, or cooking meat, which is where the dwarves come in, masters of the forge. They will braise a rack of ribs that if you weren't in the Celestial Realm, you would think you died and went to Heaven." She frowned. "That is an expression on your world, right? I'm sorry, I have been reading up on it, but I am but an amateur on your customs."

I nodded, as one of the elves slid a salad under my nose, and a dwarf followed with a seared lamb shank. I dug into both and couldn't decide which was better. "They are both phenomenal."

"Indeed," Frigg said. "You can just magic yourself some food of course, but if you're going to eat, then I say go all out. Besides, I always felt like food prepared by magic had an odd aftertaste."

I couldn't sit because my cocktail dress was too tight, so I bent my entire upper body over the plate to eat, careful not to stain the uncomfortable seams that dug into either side of my chest. No amount of beauty was worth this kind of torture.

"I feel like I'm going to pop a seam in this dress," I said, which was met with a chuckle from Frigg. "And I wouldn't want to insult Odin by busting out of it in front of him."

"Are you kidding, my dear?" Frigg said. "He would love that. It's not like he gets much action these days...and I mean that in every sense of the word."

The kitchen staff all looked off into space as if they didn't want to acknowledge Frigg's comment, and I was torn between laughing and staying dead faced. After all, I was here to convince Frigg of my worth as much as her husband, and if I didn't make a good impression on her, then I wouldn't even get a chance to make my case to Odin.

"That's a shame, because you have a smokin' body."

I regretted my words the minute they came out of my mouth. The kitchen staff turned to Frigg to judge her expression. She was stone-faced for a moment, and then another uncomfortable one, before her lips curled into a smile.

"Well, aren't you sweet?"

"I haven't ever, not once, been called that by anybody but Rose."

"Is she your paramour?" Frigg asked in a breathy, ethereal voice.

"Yeah, she is."

"How nice."

I smiled at her and realized that I had been holding my breath, waiting for her reaction. "There's one thing I love about you gods. It's that you are very accommodating to who we humans love."

"I don't understand."

"Well, on Earth—let's just say there are lots of people who don't accept Rose and my relationship, including her parents."

Her brow furrowed. "That is baffling to me. My friend Loki once had a relationship with a horse and it seemed to make him very happy, so who am I to judge?"

"Literally a god," I replied. "If you aren't qualified to judge, then who is?"

"Exactly."

"That's real progressive of you, Frigg, especially considering how you gods seem to judge everything else us humans do."

This time my words were not received with nearly as much cheerfulness. Her eyes narrowed, and her lips pursed from their smile into a cold stare. "And what is that supposed to mean?"

"N-nothing. I was just talking. I didn't mean anything by it."

"How rude." She stepped forward. "I brought you into my home. I fed you, and you insult me."

I shook my head. The kitchen was quiet enough you could hear a pin drop, except nobody would dare do something that rude. "I wasn't insulting you. I was just making an observation about how nice it was you were so accommodating. It's something I don't see a lot on Earth. It wasn't an insult."

She eyed me up and down as I noted how her pleasant

demeanor turned on a dime. After a long minute, she stood up straight. "Very well, but I warn you. That kind of comment will win you no favors among the gods, and like it or not, if Rama wants allies, that is what you are after."

"I-I'm sorry. Rama told me to behave, and I stuck my foot in my mouth. It won't happen again."

"See that it doesn't." She looked toward the door. "Now, finish up. I believe it's time to take you to my husband."

I stood up straight. "I'm not hungry anymore, miss."

"Good," she replied. "You could stand to lose a few pounds. Now, let's away. Don't dawdle." She looked over at one of the more hunched dwarves. "And clean this place up. It looks frightful."

She banged one of the pots hanging over a long island on her way out, and the kitchen staff hopped to attention, rushing around with reckless intent.

CHAPTER 37

RED

"You son of a—!" I screamed, rushing Rama and slamming into him with my fists. His rock-hard body didn't move an inch, until after several blows he grabbed me by my wrists and held me back. "Unhand me, vermin!"

"Not until you calm down," he said calmly. "Remember, we talked about this, how you needed to trust me. I even warned you that you will see things that you don't like before the end."

"I didn't think you meant being in bed with the enemy," I growled, trying my best to pull my arms free.

"I'm not the enemy," Brahma said out of the face on the right side of his head. It spun to the center. "But since you believe that, I must have played my part rather well, if I do say so myself." His head spun again. "Yes, I think we've done an excellent job."

I took a deep breath. "You can let me go now."

"Are you going to behave?"

I looked between the apsara, Rama, and Brahma. Even if they were the scum of the Earth, they were still my best chance at freedom. "Are you enemies of Zeus?"

"I would say we have a caustic relationship, but a working one," Brahma said, before his head spun once again. "And I would say we hate him."

"You know my relationship with the god of lightning," Rama said. "I had no love for him before he attacked my favorite bar, and now, I loathe him all the more."

"Any enemy of my enemy is a friend of mine, I suppose," I snarled. Rama, seemingly satisfied, let me go.

Brahma turned to his desk, but the head on the back of him spoke. "Then we have an accord, because I have no great love for humanity in general, either. Or you specifically. You are a means to an end for us, and we would be silly not to use it."

"And what exactly are you asking me to do?" I asked.

"Rama said you were smart. I would have thought you put it together already. Perhaps he was mistaken."

I rubbed my right wrist, trying to regain feeling in it. "I have my assumptions, but I want to hear it from your mouth."

"Why don't you tell me what you think, and then I will tell you whether you are right or wrong?" All three of Brahma's faces looked smug and I wanted nothing more than to wipe that condescending look off their faces. "I think that sounds like a capital idea."

I shook my head. "I don't play games. I would rather return to my cell to rot than tell you anything." I turned to the door. "So, if you would be so kind as to lead me back there, I have a rich inner life to get back to."

Rama slid in front of it to stop me from leaving. "Please, Red."

"Don't call me that." I pushed his chiseled chest. "That's a term of endearment my friends call me."

"That's a bit harsh, don't you think?" Rama replied. "After all, I have been working to free you."

"It's true," Brahma chimed in. "I've rarely seen him work so hard at anything, and I have known him for eons."

I moved toward Rama with harsh, violent steps. "You got me into this mess in the first place, so saving me doesn't win you any points in my book. Getting me free is the absolute least you can do." I turned to Brahma. "And in the second place, neither of you would be helping me if you didn't have something to gain from it, and I know one thing about friends: They don't have ulterior motives."

"Fine, Gabrielle," Rama said in a huff. "Can I at least call you Gabby?"

"No!" I barked. "Now, if there is nothing else, then—"

"We want you to kill Zeus," Brahma said, quietly and dignified. "Only a human can do it, and you are supposedly the most talented that Rama has ever seen."

I inhaled slowly on my way to the table. "There you go. I knew that Rama was testing me for some purpose, and now I know what it is."

"Actually, when we met I didn't know what purpose you would serve, just that Nox favored you and had created your body from the ether. This is just a fortuitous turn of events that brings you together with the means to destroy our greatest rival."

"And what happens with Zeus dead?" I asked. "What's to stop him from being a martyr?"

"That's where we come in," Brahma said. "With Zeus dead, I use my connections to appoint Odin to fill his seat temporarily, and then, together with Svarog and Ukko, we have a two-thirds majority to change things for the better."

"What about the others?" I asked.

"Without Zeus, Osiris and Tengri will not be able to

maintain their stalemate with the more reformist faction of the Council."

I sat down across from Brahma. "And what would you reform, exactly?"

"All of it, or at least the bits that don't directly interfere with me maintaining some semblance of control over the universe."

I pursed my lips and looked at Rama. "And you approve of this?"

He sat down next to me. "It's not quite the complete destruction of the Board I had hoped for, but it's better than where it stands now, especially if we can get Odin on our side."

"And how are you going to do that?"

Rama smiled. "I have Chelle meeting with him right now. Hopefully, we will have a diplomatic solution imminently."

"Oh, great," I replied. "She's always been really good at diplomacy." I stopped for a moment. "That was sarcasm."

"It's not ideal," Rama said. "But we are doing what is best with what we have."

"And in order for this to work, you need Zeus dead?" I smirked. "I have to say I like the sound of that. But I don't trust you in the least. There are all sorts of reasons you could want Zeus dead, and the accumulation of power is its own reward."

"Without power, we cannot change things for the better," Rama said. "I will not deny that I covet power, but I believe my motivations to be pure, in this instance."

I studied Brahma. "And what about you? Are your motives pure?"

"As the driven snow." He nodded. "I cannot say I agree

with everything Rama says, but as for now, we are aligned, as much as any gods can be at any one time."

"I can't believe I'm saying this, but that's good enough for me," I finally said. The three of us continued to stare at one another for a long moment. "How do we do this?"

"Oh, good. I was worried we would have to use other methods to convince you," one of Brahma's heads said before spinning to another one. "You came to us with a golden dagger, a rare weapon that can kill a god, but only if wielded by a human. We will assist you in stealing the dagger back from the armory, and then you will use it to kill Zeus."

Finally, I smirked. "I have to admit, I really want to tell you to pound sand, but the chance to kill Zeus and save Nox is too good an opportunity to pass up. I'm in, but if you screw me then I'll come for you next."

Brahma laughed. "I would expect nothing less."

CHAPTER 38

ARIEL

Vivian led us back out of the vault and laid herself on the bed that she and Nox had apparently shared many times before. A mournful sigh came from her as she ran her fingers into the grooves her lover once curled into next to her. "I trust you."

"Are you sure this will work?"

She shrugged. "Nox did the same spell for me a dozen times. Just say the words exactly as I told you, and it will be fine. Like I said, I trust you."

"I don't know why you would," I said. "I've never even tried to invade somebody's thoughts and dreams before."

"You're going to do great. Just put me under and then find me inside my mind."

"Oh, that sounds easy."

"For me it's as easy as falling asleep." She smiled. "Just relax. You have got this. The power is literally inside of you."

"You have a lot of faith in me," I replied, placing my hands on either side of her temple. "*Somnum.*"

Vivian's breathing fell into a deep rhythm as her eyes

closed and she drifted off to sleep. That was the easy part. Now, I had to make her remember the correct memory and find her in her dreams. I looked over at the desk she told me Nox had used, and thought hard about what I wanted her to remember. "*Memento.*"

I laid down next to her and placed one hand on her forehead while another rested on my temple. "I hope this works. *Somnum.*"

I was guided with nothing but my instincts, and I hoped they would lead me to her in her dreams. Those same instincts brought me to Nox's castle and allowed me to survive Vivian's attacks. How far we had come, from battling each other to trusting each other, in a matter of hours.

That was my last thought as my eyes grew heavy and I fell to sleep. In the darkness of my mind, I fell and fell. I couldn't remember the last time I'd slept. It was a luxury in the Dream Realm, as our entire existence was a dream.

The ground came upon me fast, but my body slowed and I touched onto the wet ground softly. Nox was speaking to my sister, staring up at the stars.

"Where are we?" I asked.

"This was our first date, if you can call it that," Vivian said. Her dream self stood on two legs. "She told me she could see the whole of the cosmos in my eyes, and then showed it all to me. I had never seen anything as beautiful as that night sky. It almost made me wish I could walk on land so I could see it every night."

"I'm surprised to hear you say that, given how much animosity you have for my people."

"Jealousy, too," Vivian replied. "It is heresy to pine for the surface world, and I have hated myself every day since then. However, I can't deny there is beauty in it, just like there is in the bottom of the ocean. Can we please get out of here?"

"Yes, I think I overshot my target." I placed my hand on her head. "I need you to think of the cave, and then, maybe I can take us there."

Vivian closed her eyes tightly. After a moment, she nodded. "Okay. I have it."

I touched the sides of her head. "*Memento.*"

The world lurched and broke apart, reforming into the cave, complete with the closed vault as we stared at the empty desk. From the left, I heard giggling, and when I turned, I saw Nox and Vivian wrapped around each other, tangled in the covers of her bedding.

"Oh!" I said, covering my eyes. "No, no, no. I don't want to see this."

She smiled. "Sorry, this is the memory that stood out to me. The first time we—"

"Don't want to know," I muttered. "Let's just get out of here. Can you please focus?"

She giggled. "Sorry. I'm ready."

I placed my hands on her head and whispered the spell. This time instead of breaking apart, the world sped up, going black and then fading in with each time Vivian came to see Nox until—

"Stop!" Vivian shouted. "There!"

The world slowed down around us. "I remember this day. I came early and surprised her." We watched her dream self emerge from the water. Nox's face contorted in surprise and she picked up the ledger immediately, murmuring something.

"What did she say?" I asked.

Vivian leaned closer. "*Per velamen.*"

"Are you sure?"

She nodded as the book vanished. "Clear as day."

"Then let's get out of here." I snapped my fingers. "*Expergisci!*"

My eyes fluttered open, and I turned over to see Vivian wake up. It registered with me that she and Nox had shared this bed, and I jumped up when I realized I was laying in the same groove Nox had laid.

"You are such a prude," Vivian said, standing with a stretch.

"I am not. I just don't want to think of my sister...doing that."

"Well, we're not really sisters, right?"

I shook the shivers off me. "Still, I would rather not have that rattling around my brain."

"Get over it." She walked over to the desk. "Besides, we got what we needed. You should be happy. Let's see if it worked."

I held my hand over the place where I watched Nox place the book through the air. "*Per velamen.*"

The air seemed to tear, and I felt something thick and heavy in my hand. I yanked it through the veil into our dimension and threw it on the desk. Sure enough, it was a book, and when I flipped it open, it held thousands of entries with all sorts of items, with locations and dates.

"Perfect," Vivian said with a smirk. "Now, let's go find that eye."

"And mother's trident," I added.

"Of course," she said. "That too."

CHAPTER 39
NIMUE

"Are you going to be okay?" I asked Delilah "You can stay longer, if you need to."

She stood in the doorway. "Thank you, but this is too much socializing in one day for me. And no, I am not okay, and I likely won't be ever again, but you have been kind."

"It was nothing."

She grabbed my hands. "It was not nothing." She sped away, her dress stained with Hastur's violence.

I closed the door and leaned against it. I wasn't lying that Delilah could have stayed as long as she wanted, but a large part of me was glad she left. I was exhausted in a way I hadn't been in a long time. I took another swig of the black ichor and laid in bed. When I turned, I left a bloodstain on the sheets from where my skinless body came in contact with the sheets.

I had forgotten what a monster I had become. I thought about the days I'd spent with my friend and roommate Gwen, before sleeping with her boyfriend—then killing him—and taking over the Unseelie Court. We used to sit up late, watch bad movies, and talk about the future. What would that young girl think of me now, a shell of my former self, forced to grovel to a king to recover my skin?

It was too much to consider, so instead I laid my head down on the pillow, and allowed myself, for the first time in weeks, to drift off to sleep.

"I found you," The Faceless Woman's voice crackled in the darkness, and then, in a flash, she crashed at my feet. "My godless dear, what has he done to you?"

"Nothing that you didn't allow," I replied. "You abandoned me, Rapunzel."

"I did not allow any of this. You were lost to me, and I cried out to find you. The King in Yellow is crafty and tricksy. He hid you from me by holding sleep from you, and now, I can only imagine he has let you free for some purpose."

"I am not free," I replied. "However, he has granted me a reprieve from my pain, in order to test if I am worthy to become his consort."

"One of his monsters, you mean."

"No, one of his princesses. They are not monsters. They are beautiful and haunted. Prisoners, just like me." My words were bitter. I had grown to care for Delilah and the others during my time in the castle. "There are monsters here, but the princesses are not them."

"They have warped you, but I have run out of patience with this discussion. I have only one question. How did you fail?"

"Yes, why would you ask how I am doing? That would be too much for you." I sighed. "Your precious Cassandra betrayed me. I trusted her because you trusted her, and she turned on me without a second thought."

"That is troubling, but not wholly surprising." Rapunzel thought for a moment. "She was lost for a long time, and I thought I brought her back to sanity, but I could never give her the one thing she wanted, the return of her skin."

"She has taken mine, and it hangs off of her."

"It is a cruel punishment for you both. You, of course, but also for her—it must cause her grief to have the skin she's wanted for so long, only it doesn't fit her body."

"At least she has skin."

Rapunzel stepped closer. "You can have it, if you complete the task and kill the king like we planned."

I scoffed. "You couldn't help Cassandra. Why would I believe you can help me?"

"The reason I couldn't help her is because his magic is glued to her. If he died, I would be able to overpower it finally, and give her, and you, back what you so desire."

"I desire more than my skin, Rapunzel. I desire power and strength. The kind that comes with ruling."

"Then you are considering his offer?" Rapunzel asked slowly, disappointment oozing from her words.

"I am considering all possibilities and deciding whom to give my allegiance."

"It is folly to trust him after what he has done to you."

"And what have you done for me? You gave me your blessing and look at what it's gotten me. I am trapped in a castle, enemies around every turn. If you were truly power-ful, you would save me, instead of sitting on your hands."

"I can't do that. Not while he has a piece of my face. If you would get it for me—"

"It's always what I can do for you. All of you with power are the same. You will only help once the powerless have served you."

Her tone grew more menacing. "You made a deal with Baba. Did you forget that?"

"And she is free to collect any time. I would welcome

her torture at this point. But she does not come for me, which proves neither of you have power here."

"If you turn your back on me, it is a slight I will not forget."

"I have angered more powerful beings than you in my time. If you think I fear you, then you can come and face me at any time. Now, get out of my head."

I snapped my fingers and my eyes popped open. I did not like upsetting Rapunzel. I already had to deal with Hastur, and I had no interest in having another powerful being on my bad side, but there was no doubt it was a trap. I hoped I played my part well enough to please my master and have him pull me closer into his orbit.

CHAPTER 40

ROSE

Rama's portal spat me out into a dingy alley in a rainstorm. The drops scalded my skin.

"*Praesidium.*" A force field created a barrier around my body, but still the acid rain bounced from the asphalt and ate at my shoes and pants. I ran into the first building I could see, one with a red door.

"My gods, lady." A burly man in a white shirt stepped out from behind a red curtain. "Don't you know not to be caught out in a storm?"

Gods bless the fact that Hypnos and Persephone's blessings combined to give me a perfect understanding of foreign languages, because otherwise I would be screwed when trying to understand him.

I dropped my hand from over my head and shook off the spell, trying to think quickly of a palatable lie. "I didn't expect it to start for a few hours."

"You must be really confident, because I would not be caught dead outside with a storm brewing like this one."

"Is it supposed to rain long?"

He chuckled. "At least until tomorrow morning. Do you have an ID?"

I patted my shirt, looking for one hidden in a pocket, but came up empty. "Maybe they were eaten by the storm."

"Then I guess you can't pay cover, can you?"

I grimaced. "I can clean dishes or something."

"You must not know what this place is, or you wouldn't say, 'or something.' " When I looked at him cock-eyed, he just laughed. "Go inside. I'll cover you."

"Really?"

"Sure, but no touching," he said. "You look like the touching type."

I didn't understand what he meant until I walked through the curtain and saw that it was a strip club. Women danced and gyrated all over the bar, on men that generally looked like they were on loan from a prison, mixed with ones who were out to spend their lunch break in style.

Before I could walk inside, the bouncer pushed through the curtain. "Buffet is free, and it's pretty good. Come on. Let's get some food in you, waif."

I stepped past a stripper pole, and then a second one, before curving around a man getting a lap dance, and up to a table filled with fried chicken, rice, and thin ribs, along with something that resembled mashed potatoes, gravy, and mushy spinach. The bouncer made a plate for himself, and I followed his lead, taking only what he deemed worthwhile.

"Why are you being nice to me?" I asked him.

"Why shouldn't I be nice? Are you a bad person?"

"No, but...people aren't usually so nice."

He walked down from the buffet. "Come on."

"Have you worked here long?" I asked.

"Too long," he said. "But it's decent pay, and I do have a thing for titties."

He didn't ogle or objectify me, though. Instead, he led me to a table in the back and sat with me as I ate.

I hadn't realized how hungry I was. I dug in. "You're right, this is good."

"Come for the boobies. Stay for the foodies." He chuckled. "I tried to pitch that once as a promo, but they said naked women were enough of a promo."

"I think your slogan's pretty good, personally."

After eating a couple of ribs, he sat back and wiped his mouth with a napkin. "So, you have magic, huh?"

I nearly choked on my mashed potatoes. "What? What makes you think that? That's ridiculous."

"I saw you walking across the street, and I got eyes." He held up his hand. "Don't worry. This is a safe space. The Greckos don't come around here often, and we pay them handsomely to look the other way when they do."

"Who are the Greckos?"

He laughed. "You really aren't from around here."

I shook my head. "I'm not. I'm from...somewhere else. I'm looking for somebody, and my friend said I might be able to find her here."

"It's possible. Lots of girls pass through here. Who are you looking for?"

I swallowed my food and looked up at him. "Her name is Kadlu."

Now, it was his turn to choke on his food. When he recovered, his face turned cold. "Get out."

"Excuse me?"

He pulled my plate away from me. "We don't want any of your kind of trouble here. This is a respectable establishment. Now get out."

"But—"

"Get out, or I'll call the Greckos on you right now."

I stood up. "I'm sorry to have offended you."

"You'll be sorry for a lot more if you don't turn around and walk away right now. There's a shelter two streets down. Maybe they'll take in magical strays, but I wouldn't say that name willy-nilly if you know what's good for you."

"I—" It was no use arguing. "Thank you."

He hesitated for half a second and pursed his lips. "Ask for Andie. She's kinder than I am."

With that, I passed through the tables, swerving my way out of the club, with every eye on me as I went. I didn't know what I'd done, but something told me this was going to be much harder than I thought—and I already thought it would be impossible.

I passed a bucket full of metallic, oversized umbrellas, and stole a tall one with a wooden handle before storming off into the rain.

CHAPTER 41

ARIEL

"It's over here!" I shouted. We were rushing down the bleach-white aisles of Nox's vault. The harsh light thrumming from the floor to ceiling made it hard to focus or maintain a sense of direction, but the longer we navigated the corridors, the easier it became to deal with the constant pulse of the lights. They laid so evenly that they prevented even shadows from forming, and I realized it was likely an intended feature, to continually disorient intruders.

We finally came upon a long wooden box with a trident burned into it. According to Nox's ledger, it was the Trident of Atlantis that Vivian had been searching for all this time.

"Mother has been trying to recover this for as long as she has been queen." Vivian flipped the box's latches carefully and methodically, looking for traps. "She will be so pleased with me when I bring it to her."

"And me as well," I replied, expectantly. "I hope she will see that I am not a threat to her rule, but a boon."

"I promise to do justice to you, my sister," Vivian said, opening the box. The stark yellow glow from inside it clashed with the soft white of the rest of the room, and cast strange shadows against the walls. For a moment, I swore I saw two eyes looking out from one of them, but it disappeared when Vivian pulled the staff from the box.

She held the trident up in the air, and something pulsed through my body. It wasn't painful, but it was powerful, and it emanated from Vivian's aura. The trident no longer glowed but shimmered in the light.

Vivian slammed the butt of the trident on the ground, and a small quake rippled from her and knocked me off balance. She smiled. "Marvelous."

She studied the golden spikes that made up the trident's forks, breathing heavily and smiling. She spun the shaft in her hands until the different colored gems converged into a single white light that shot out across the vault.

"Okay," I said. "Enough playing. Do you think you can use that trident to help us find the eye or not?"

Even though we had the ledger and a location for Rapunzel's eye, it wasn't easy to find. With hundreds of columns and rows, and a numbering system that seemed to be indecipherable to any but Nox, we could search for days and not come up with the location. Our locator spells didn't seem to work in the vault, either, likely a failsafe from a paranoid god.

"Do you find it weird that a god of darkness would keep a vault guarded by the light?" Vivian asked.

"I suppose so," I said. "I hadn't really thought about it."

"No, of course you didn't." Her tone was condescending, and I had to stifle my desire to punch her in the face. "You are only human, after all. I have been thinking about it for a long time. Why would she choose light to guard her most precious secrets?" She was nearly on top of me. "Open to the page."

I flipped the book to where we had found the entry for the eye. "There it is."

"Excellent," Vivian said, clearing her throat and holding her arms wide. "Nox taught me many things over the years, but the most powerful was how to control the darkness. I never could get the shadows to bend to my will, even with all my power. However, with this trident, I believe I can do so."

"Well, make it quick then," I said. "Enough blustering."

She cleared her throat and tapped the trident on the page. "Great darkness, shroud of the truth of the universe. Guide me to the item I seek. Use me to do your mistress's will and let her love for you flow through me."

Nothing happened.

I threw my hands in the air and spun on the spot. "Great, now we're back to square one. I should have known that shadows couldn't—"

With a great show of force, Vivian convulsed, and shadows shot from her body and through the trident. They plumed into the air and condensed into a thin stream. With a jolt, they snaked across the ground. Instantly, we followed the path laid out by the shadows.

"Why is this working?" I asked.

"It makes perfect sense to me." Vivian's eyes still leaked black shadows. "Nox controls darkness, but very few gods are comfortable delving into that side of magic. They prefer the light, because it is 'pretty,' even if it is vapid, or maybe because it is. Regardless, knowing this preference, Nox designed her vault to consume the light, rendering it powerless. The vault will reveal its magic only to her darkness, and only it can withstand the ceaseless brightness of this place."

"I don't get it," I said flatly. "But magic never made

much sense to me."

"It's not supposed to. That's the beauty of it."

The dark path splintered from the main line and crept into the corners of the vault, giving shadow and finding solace in the nooks and crannies of Nox's treasures. With the new variations in the light, objects filled out with depth and weight where there had been none, and I appreciated the complexity of their designs. I had simply passed over them before.

"There!" Vivian shouted. We followed the shadows to a point in the floor where it all gathered, blotting out the white light and replacing it with darkness.

The shadows coalesced on the third shelf of an unassuming bookcase where there was a shining, red box carved with runes. I looked over at Vivian, who nodded, and I picked it up. The box was cool to the touch, but I felt a vibration inside, like the same power Vivian had just displayed when she wielded the trident.

"I think this is it," I breathed.

"Well, open it up and find out," Vivian replied. "Don't just stand there like an idiot."

I ignored her insult and opened the case. The stench of death plumed out, and I choked on the air. I nearly dropped the box. When I recovered, I peered down into the box and saw a round eye, veiny and still, with the sinew still attached. The purple iris looked up at me, motionless.

"Well, this is an eye, all right." I looked over at the book, and then at the number labeled underneath the box. "And these numbers match, so this has to be it."

"Good," Vivian said, leveling the trident at me. "Now is the point where I betray you. Thank you so much for not making me swear an oath to a magical binding. That would have complicated things."

CHAPTER 42

CHELLE

Frigg didn't speak again after we left the kitchen. I had clearly offended her, and even though I took every chance to apologize, her face was stoic. It reminded me of my own father, who could materialize the smallest slight as a vendetta and use it to give you the silent treatment for weeks, until you were almost sure he would never talk again, and then he would smile sweetly like nothing happened.

"Stay here," Frigg said abruptly. She disappeared behind a pair of wooden doors carved with trees and squirrels.

Odin was behind the door, no doubt. I wondered what she would tell him. I'd told Rama I was no diplomat, and here I was, having royally screwed things up. If Odin really was critical to the reconstruction of the Celestial Realm and the direction of the cosmos, then Frigg telling him what a terrible person I was would surely doom our cause. I hoped he wouldn't disintegrate me on sight, and that I could leave with my life, if not my dignity.

It took several minutes of me pacing the foyer, shoes

clacking on the floor as I tried desperately not to fall—which at least offered me a distraction—before a small man opened the door. He was made of clay, with empty sockets where his eyes should be. Instead of calling out, he simply turned and walked back into the room. I didn't know if I should follow, but I assumed as much, and the disgruntled face of the clay man when I entered told me I should have come sooner.

The golem was half my size but walked faster than I could follow. If I thought the foyer was garish, it was nothing compared to the intricately detailed antechamber he led me through. Wood paneling on the arched walls was carved with birds that seemed to soar toward you as you moved past. Statues of bears, wolves, and all manner of creature I didn't recognize were erected around the room, so lifelike I swore they moved and growled at me.

Without a word, the golem motioned me through a door into a cold and dark room. When the door closed, two shafts of light came down from the ceiling. One illuminated Frigg, sitting on a throne of oak and green velvet; the other showed an old man with a patch over his left eye, scowling.

"So, you are the one whom Rama sent me," the man barked, gripping the edges of his throne so tightly his knuckles were white.

I knelt. "You must be Odin. I am honored to meet you."

"Bah!" Odin cried. "I don't care about your well-words. Show me the power child."

"The power...?" I frowned. "I'm afraid I don't know what you mean."

"You are part of Nox's secret weapon, are you not? Meant to usher the universe into a new age of beauty and bravery?"

"I don't—"

"Well, let's see it." Odin slammed his hands against the edges of his chair, causing the whole room to vibrate. "Otherwise, this is all a waste of time."

"I know some magic," I said. "But compared to your greatness, they would be little more than parlor tricks, Your Grace."

"I don't think you understand," Frigg said, giving me a cold look. "Present your power, or Lord Odin will destroy you."

"I tire of this!" Odin nearly squealed. It was not becoming of a god, but I was frightened of how unhinged he was. At any second, he could pull the universe apart and rip me from it.

"Okay," I said. I took a deep breath and thought of the most powerful spell I could think of. *"Fulgur tempestas!"*

I brought my hands down and a lightning storm descended, crashing into the floor and chipping the marble.

Odin did not move. "Another!"

"Magna augue!" This time a giant fireball appeared above my outstretched hands. I threw it at Frigg, and she caught it with one hand, a bored look on her face.

"Anything else?" she asked.

There was one other spell I could cast. I hadn't done it in a long time because it always scared me, but I needed something that would impress even a god. *"Solem ignis!"*

I brought my hands up and created a miniature sun that grew until it filled half the room. My fear was that I would lose control of it—not an unfounded one, since I had once almost destroyed my house using it.

"That will be quite enough," Frigg said.

I tried to stop it, but I couldn't. "I can't—"

Odin growled and stomped his foot on the ground. The quake shot through the floors and my sun dissipated.

He waved a hand in disgust. "I thought she would be powerful."

"Perhaps she doesn't know how to use her power. We should experiment on her still, and make sure that she is what she claims." Frigg gave me an appraising look. "She has already been drugged, after all. It would be a shame to let that go to waste."

"Excuse me?" I said, but the air became heavy, and my legs wiggled underneath me. I tried to move forward, to raise my arms, but everything felt like a million pounds. All I could do under the weight was fall, cracking my head on the floor and passing into unconsciousness.

CHAPTER 43

RED

"You need to be quick," Rama said as he finished laying out the plan to steal back the weapon from the armory. The Board kept a stash there of the most important weapons they had confiscated from across the universe. Brahma, Rama, the apsara and I had been going over it for an hour, and Rama waited until we were done to add a little bit of fuel to the fire. "I need that dagger."

"It's my dagger. How can you need my dagger?"

"To save the universe, of course," Rama said. "I thought that was what we were all fighting for."

I shook my head. "I'm fighting for my freedom, and my friends. The universe can suck noodles for all I care."

Rama smirked. "Then you should be quick for the sake of your friends, because they are in a lot of trouble. If you will not do it for the universe, then at least do it for them."

"Leave my friends alone, Rama," I growled, stepping toward him.

"I'm trying to help them." He held up his hands. "Are you that dense? We need your help to save them."

"And I'm sure you didn't have anything to do with their

condition," I replied. "Just like you had nothing to do with getting me captured."

"I have taken responsibility for my part in your capture and am trying to help you escape. I'm simply telling you the stakes, should you fail."

"I was going to succeed either way, but now, you might just find a golden dagger in your own heart once this is said and done."

"Please," Brahma said with a sigh, leaning his elbows on his desk. "Can we please focus on the prize of killing Zeus?"

"That may be your prize," I said. "But mine is freedom —for myself, for Nox, and for my friends."

Brahma waved his hand. "Fine, fine, but none of that happens without Zeus's death. He is holed up in his office for another hour, which is just about the amount of time it will take for Athena to find out you are gone. If you are to succeed, then it must be now or never."

I squared my shoulders and turned to the door of Brahma's office. "I vote now."

The apsara walked to the door. "I will guide you through the halls. Stay close to me and you will remain cloaked to all who wish to do you harm."

"Just get me out of here," I said as she opened the door. "I can't take this testosterone anymore."

The plan was relatively simple: The armory was guarded by a patrol of crystal golems, angels, Valkyrie, Devas, and minor deities. Once I got through them, I'd find the weapons stored in caches behind thick metal bars. Luckily, Brahma was on the Board, and was able to find both the location of the cache and its key. Assuming I could get inside, I needed to get to the cache and retrieve my golden dagger. From there, I could take an air duct to Zeus's laboratory, where I would be able to stab him in the chest with the dagger and kill him. Rama would save Nox and we would escape into the bowels of the Sanctuary to freedom.

The apsara was shockingly good at going unnoticed. She walked lightly without her shoes, and only revealed herself when absolutely necessary, or to others who were friendly to her. She had built up a network of trusted people throughout the Sanctuary and a flawless map of those whose help she could obtain. She slipped through doors at just the right moment, forcing me to leap and strain to keep up with her movements. While she let me in on her secrets sometimes, most of the time I simply followed her lead, like a dance where the lead was unpredictable and uncommunicative.

"Stop," she whispered when we'd maneuvered through the Sanctuary. She ducked behind a wall. "The door behind that guard is the armory."

I peeked my head around the wall and saw two angels standing in front of a large, black, metal door. It was more advanced than the ancient tech guarding the rest of the facility. Part of me thought that the reason why we'd gotten as far as we had was because the gods didn't believe anyone would dare challenge them, so they saw no need for technology to help protect them.

Now, with the door behind the hulking angels, I saw that I was wrong. "Do you have the keycode?"

The apsara nodded. "I do, but I need to provide the distraction for you. When I pull the guards away from the door, use the code 2-4-9-7-5-1-3-6-8 and slip inside. You will only have a moment, so use it well."

I nodded and the apsara strode into the open. The angels didn't take notice of her at first, but then she reached into her pocket and put on her shoes. They clacked loudly and revealed her, so that the guards went into high alert, rushing forward to pepper her with questions.

In the chaos, she managed to get their backs to the door. Their shouts hid the noise of me plugging in the code and slipping inside. With the door closed, I still heard their muffled shouts, but my body relaxed from the threat of the guards seeing me.

"Who are you?" a gruff voice demanded.

I turned to see a tubby but still broad Valkyrie swinging a scimitar. I ducked the blow and rolled across the metal grates. I went for my throwing daggers on instinct, forgetting they'd been taken from me.

I couldn't let the Valkyrie call to his brethren. I leapt for his arm, spinning his scimitar toward him and stabbing it into his chest. The Valkyrie slid against the wall as blood gurgled from the open wound. I pulled the scimitar from his hand and turned to the caches of weapons.

His death complicated things and meant I needed to move faster. I had memorized the location of the golden dagger and hastened over to it. Using the key Brahma gave me, I unlocked the metal bars and slid inside, where I found several big wooden boxes. I used the scimitar to pry open each one until I found one that made me smile. Inside was my cape and the collection of my weapons, including, of course, the golden dagger.

I threw them on as quickly as possible, sliding the cape over my shoulders and my daggers into their position on my belt before I heard the guards scream out from the front of the armory.

"Somebody's here! Sound the alarm!"

Crap.

CHAPTER 44
ROSE

The man from the strip club had said, "Two streets down," which could have meant literally anything since the club was situated on a street corner. I trudged down each street in three different directions, all while acid rain ate through the metal sheen of the umbrella, before I finally found the Seventh Street Animal Shelter. I wondered for a minute if I should try the fourth direction but figured that the rain would eat clean through the umbrella before long, so it was the animal shelter or nothing.

The door was closed and covered by a thick, white grate. When I rang the bell, I heard a cacophony of barks and squeaks and squawks, among other less pleasant and unfamiliar sounds. I stood anxiously under the precarious overhang waiting for an answer while the rain kicked up on my legs. The droplets had eaten through the soles of my shoes and the bottoms of my pants, making them more like ragged capris than anything. Finally, the call box crackled to life with a loud buzz.

"We're closed," a woman's voice growled. "Get your food somewhere else, junkie."

I pressed the call box. "I'm not a junkie. I was sent here by a bouncer at the"—*what was the name of the club?* I passed it so many times. There was a neon sign with a cat blinking in and out in green and pink—"Cat Scratch Nightclub."

"You a stripper?"

"No. I'm looking for Andie. He said she could help me."

There was another long silence, and then the call box buzzed again. "Come in. Close the door and take the stairs to your right up two flights. I'll holler when I hear you coming."

The door cracked open with another loud buzz, and I scooted inside, closing the door and pushing against it just to be sure it was locked. I thought for a minute that it might not be a good idea to lock myself in with whomever was upstairs, but I couldn't take one more second in the acid rain, so I decided to take my chances. Besides, I had magic.

I placed my ratty shoes next to the others which were in considerably better shape and started up the stairs. My soggy socks slapped against every step until I finally took them off at the first landing. They were eaten to shit anyway, and the water lodged in them burned my skin.

The lights were mostly off on the third floor, save for a few rickety overhead lights that swung from thick cords overhead, filling the hallway with a combination of green, sickly light, and oppressive darkness.

"Third door on the left!" I recognized the voice from the intercom, though considerably less garbled.

A white light shone under the door, telling me that somebody was inside. I pushed it open slowly and found both barrels of a shotgun pointing at me.

"Hello, sweetheart."

The woman sat at a desk, brown hair pulled back in a

tight ponytail, and motioned with the gun to a rickety chair across from her. "Why don't you sit down and tell me why Yrzon would send you to me?"

"Are you Andie, then?" I asked as I slid into the chair. "You really don't need that gun."

"I'll tell you what I need," she replied. "And yeah, I am Andie."

"It's a pleasure to meet you, even with the gun. Thank you for letting me in out of the rain."

"I'd say it was my pleasure, but that would be a lie." Andie's eyes narrowed. "Are you an idiot, girl?"

I shook my head. "I don't think so, but then, maybe that's why I keep getting into these situations."

"You have to be an idiot, miss thing, because only an idiot would be wandering outside in an acid rainstorm." She moved the gun out of the way and studied my face. "You're pretty for an idiot."

"Thank you," I replied. "I don't see what that has to do with anything, though."

"It doesn't," she replied. "Just an observation. You know, people are more likely to help pretty people, and you are real pretty."

I felt my cheeks warm. "I'm not very good with compliments, but again, thank you. I hope that means you are willing to help me."

She cocked her head. "I didn't say *I* like pretty, just that people like pretty, in general. I'm personally wary of people that are too pretty because they always seem to be working both sides against the center."

"I don't—"

Andie cut me off. "How about you just tell me what you want and know that I have a skill with liars." She tapped her gun on the table. "This might be filled with rock salt, but it hurts like Hell, and it'll leave a big welt on those perfect tits of yours."

I gaped at her. "I just needed a place to get out of the rain."

She fired the shotgun over her shoulder. Clearly, it wasn't the first time she'd done so. The whole wall was peppered with holes. "That was only a half truth, but I'm afraid I'm going to need the whole of it. Where did you come from?"

"My friend's house," I stammered. "In the Celestial Realm."

Her eyes narrowed again but she nodded slowly. "Keep going. Why are you here?"

"I'm in search of someone. My friend tracked her here, to this planet. I need her help."

"Well, dagnabit. Didn't I say that you pretty folks always needed something? Son of a—" She leveled the gun at me. "I should kill you now."

"I thought that was only filled with rock salt."

"Anything is deadly in the right hands."

I smiled a small smile. "I wouldn't do that if I were you. I am being very polite, but I can assure you that I am fully capable of defending myself."

"I don't doubt it, being from the Celestial Realm and all. We don't care much for gods down here, especially after how badly you screwed everything up with your stupid little war."

"War?"

She laughed. "You really aren't from here. A hundred years ago, Svarog versus Tengri for control of our little piece of Heaven. They built up followers on both sides, and in the final battle, they decided they would rather neither of them have it, so they scorched the sky and tainted the water, figuring we would just die out. Us humans are scrappier than cockroaches though, and we found a way to live."

It didn't make sense. Why would members of the Board fight each other for control of a planet? Shouldn't they be on the same team? I pushed the questions to the back of my mind. I feared asking anything else would bring down Andie's ire, and I really didn't want to melt her face off.

"I'm so sorry to hear that."

"Not your fault, doll," Andie said. "But we don't much like gods around here, or magic. I should call the Greckos on you."

"Maybe I was mistaken," I replied, starting to stand. "I will tell my master that Kadlu is not on this planet."

Her face softened. "I...haven't heard that name in a long time. What do you want with Kadlu?"

"I have a gift for her," I said. "I know she is looking for ways to kill a god, and I happen to have one—a dagger, which a friend of mine used to kill a god, has been located." I thumbed the piece of paper as I pulled it out of my pocket. "Of course, I'm sure you have no need for something like that."

I turned to leave and I heard the gun cock before she fired again. I threw a forcefield around myself, squeezing all the rock salt until it fell to the ground as powder.

"Well, I'll be dipped. I guess you can defend yourself."

"The gods do not associate with the powerless or unordinary."

"I do," the woman said. "But then, I'm not much of a god."

Andie morphed into a dark-skinned woman with a round face and large green eyes that seemed to pierce my soul. She laid the shotgun on the table and rose from her seat.

"You stink of Rama," she growled. "Now, show me this weapon or I will disintegrate you, and then reconstitute you and do it again, until I bore of your torture and blow you into the wind."

It looked like I'd found Kadlu. It wasn't so hard, after all. Getting out alive, though, was another story.

CHAPTER 45
CHELLE

When you're born a gorgon and the whole world seems to be after you, being drugged and tricked is par for the course, so Frigg's betrayal wasn't surprising. It had been a while though, and I certainly didn't miss the headache of being drugged.

"You're awake," Odin's voice boomed from across the room. "I was hoping to finish before you woke."

I had been strapped down with thick leather and couldn't do more than glance at the bracers from the side of my eye. They were carved with runes that, I imagined, prevented people from using magic.

"I'm sorry to ruin your plans," I replied, my voice raspy.

"It's for your benefit, dear," Frigg said, walking up next to her husband. "It's quite a painful procedure, and we hoped to save you from it."

I sneered. "So, you're talking to me again, then?" I thought that I had offended her, but from the way she averted her eyes when I caught them, the truth was much more sinister. She didn't want to get too close to her test subject. "So, the food was tainted then?"

"I know it's crass, but poison is such an effective means of dealing with people. Clean and painless."

"For you, maybe," I said. "It feels like somebody cracked my head open and scooped out a big piece of my brain."

"My word," Odin said. "We'd never do something so vulgar. No, no. It's just that we don't quite believe Rama that you are as he said, and so we thought we would test for ourselves. He is asking for quite a lot, after all, and if I'm to come out of retirement then I must be sure."

"Of course." I exhaled loudly. "A powerful god like you—how could you ever recover from the humiliation if Rama tricked you?"

Odin's lips creased into an unexpected smile, and his remaining eye went wide. "That's exactly right. My, maybe I have been wrong about humanity for all these centuries if one can be as astute as you."

"I'm more astute than most, but I guess it would be nice if the gods actually cared about us, so I'll just take the compliment."

"You don't want us to care too much." He raised a syringe into the air and flicked it with his finger. "Objectivity makes us better rulers. It's not like I hate you, or anything. It's more like I nothing you." He walked over and grabbed my arm. "Now, don't fight this and it will go much quicker."

I disregarded his advice and immediately pulled as hard as I could against him, thrashing and flailing every which way. Frigg came to help her husband, putting her hands on either side of my forearm, locking me in place. Even though she seemed like a frail woman, she was still a god, and thus, more powerful than me, especially when I was restrained.

"There we go," Odin said, sticking the needle into my arm. "And now, we wait."

"Wait for what?"

"For this to make its way through your system," Frigg answered. "Then the real fun begins."

My eyes went wide. "What fun is that?"

She pointed to a small glass jar sitting on a pedestal across the room, attached to several tubes that snaked across the room. "We get to see how powerful you really are, my dear." Her brow furrowed. "I'm afraid it's not going to be as much fun for you as it is for us, though, which is why we hoped you would stay sedated."

"Yes, a sad state of affairs," Odin added.

"Oh, can't we just put her back under?" Frigg said. "She seems like a pleasant girl, though a little rough around the edges."

Odin scratched his beard. "I suppose it won't affect the results much."

"NO!" I shouted. "I don't care how painful it is. I want to know what you're doing to me."

He shrugged and picked up a pair of suction cups. "It's your funeral, as they say."

"Don't say things like that. It's a bad omen," Frigg said, then added, "I hope this doesn't kill her."

Shaking his head, Odin placed the suction cups on either side of my head, then attached the other ends of the tubes to them. "Are you very sure you want to remain awake?"

"No," I said. "I would rather you let me go, but I highly doubt that's going to happen, so yes. I want to see what you are doing to me."

"Suit yourself."

He snapped his fingers, and my entire being convulsed with pain. I wished for death but couldn't do anything except scream for a moment of salvation that never came. The only saving grace was knowing Rose didn't have to deal with this pain; it was the only thing that brought me through it.

CHAPTER 46
NIMUE

The castle staff moved through the halls like ghosts, shrinking from the walls so as not to touch anything or, gods forbid, bump into anything. They were deathly frightened of Hastur, and only slightly less so of the princesses.

I had made an impression, I hoped, on Elvira and Delilah, with Cassandra telling me she would be in my corner. There was only Bethel and Lydia, both of whom I hadn't seen since the ball, so I decided to leave my room in order to find one or, hopefully, both of them.

The first three of the princesses had been relatively easy. It took a kind word, a stern meeting, and a guilty conscience to find and ingratiate myself to them. I feared the final two would be harder to convince. Without them, my plan to slaughter Hastur had very little hope of succeeding. Elvira would only help if I could convince all of the princesses, and having all five on my side significantly increased our odds for success.

"Excuse me," I asked a ghastly thin woman carrying an armload of fresh black towels. "Do you know where Bethel or Lydia's rooms are?"

I kept my voice at a whisper, but it still frightened the poor woman, who dropped the towels she was carrying and nearly jumped out of her skin, which was something that might legitimately happen in a place like Carcosa.

"I—I—" She couldn't stop from wailing out. When I moved toward her, she leapt back. Several other servants passed by us, but they did not stop, or even acknowledge our existence.

"It's okay." I dropped down to pick up the towels. "See? Nothing is wrong. It's okay."

She shook her head until there was a crack of lightning and Lydia appeared, eyes locked on the woman. "What did you do?"

"Nothing," she said. "I didn't know that—this woman asked me a question, and it startled me."

Lydia turned to me. The universe spun where her head should have been, and when she spoke it seemed like it rattled inside my head. "Don't you know that we aren't supposed to speak to the staff? They have a job to do, and it must be done with utter perfection."

"No, no, no, no, no," the maid said. "Please, don't take my soul. I will do better."

"I'm sorry," Lydia said, holding up her hand. "I don't have a choice."

"Please! I've been here forty years and never had a slip-up until today."

"All it takes is one," Lydia's hand moved to the shaking woman. "I thought I trained you better."

"You did. You did." The women bowed to Lydia. "I am so sorry, mistress. It won't happen again—"

"Of course not." Lydia's hand filled with white hot light. "Because you will not have a chance to fail the king again."

"Are you kidding?" I growled, stepping in front of the

woman. "You are going to kill this woman because she dropped some towels?"

"Hastur requires perfection from all," Lydia said, with no fear of the name on her lips.

"That's insane!" I shouted. "I used to rule a country, and I was plenty mean in my time, but this is excessive, even for me."

"If you wish, you can take it up with the king himself. I hear he is very fond of you, and he will gladly let you suffer for this woman's mistake."

"Fine. I will do exactly that." I grabbed the woman's hand. "Come on."

The woman didn't stop whining and babbling as we walked briskly down the halls, turning this way and that, until we reached Hastur's quarters. At the King in Yellow's door, I turned to the woman. "Don't worry. It's going to be okay."

"All your skin is off," she muttered. "I don't think you have the right to say things are going to be okay."

"Fair enough," I said. "But it will be okay. If there's a punishment to be had, then it will be me that bears it."

"Why are you helping this woman?" Lydia hissed in my head. "She is nothing."

"Nobody is nothing," I replied, out loud. "I was considered a nothing once, and few looked out for me. Those that tried had no true power and were bowled over. I swore to gain power so that I would never have to feel helpless again. I know how it feels to be stomped over, and I will not let it happen to this woman because of my mistake."

I had pursued power for so long I'd forgotten the reason: to protect the defenseless, and make sure nobody could push us around. Now that I remembered, I would hold it close to me.

"You will crack," Lydia replied. "And before the end you will suffer so badly you will agree to kill this woman yourself to stop the pain."

"I'm sorry you believe that, but it's not true. I am stronger than the King in Yellow. Whatever he does to me, I will take it. I will never bring it upon this woman, or anyone else, lest they deserve it."

"And what if this woman does deserve it? She has broken the perfect system of this castle."

"If a system can be destroyed so easily, then perhaps it does not deserve to exist."

I knocked on the door, the sound echoing through the halls. There was silence for a moment, and then came a booming voice.

"Who dares disturb me?"

It was Hastur.

"It is I, Nimue, come to grovel for the life of one of your servants."

"Oh, good," Hastur replied. The door swung open, and a great gust of hot air plumed out. I thought it appropriate, given the horrible blowhard that lived inside the room "This is most fortuitous. I have need to talk to you. Please, do come in. We have much to discuss." He glanced at the others. "And bring the girl. We'll have some fun."

I grabbed the woman's hand and walked shakily into the darkness. "It's going to be okay. I promise."

"You're making a mistake," Lydia said as I disappeared.

"Then it is mine to make," I bit back, ready to face the cruel king.

CHAPTER 47

ROSE

I handed Kadlu the scrap of paper Rama had given me.

She looked at it and her eyes narrowed. "Either this is a joke, or you really messed up."

"What are you—"

She held up the piece of paper. The ink had been completely washed off, and the paper had been eaten away by the acid rain. I had failed at even the basic thing I was assigned to do.

"I'm sorry," I said. "I'm not a field agent. I shouldn't even be here. My girlf—fiancé is better at this type of thing than me."

Kadlu leaned against the side of her desk, folding her arms across her chest. "And where is this girlfriend, then?"

Her posture had relaxed slightly, but I still didn't trust that she would let me live if I didn't tell her the truth, especially after I bungled this mission. "She's trying to convince Odin to join Rama's cause."

She snorted. "I find it hard to believe that Rama believes in anything besides his own hide."

"He does, though," I replied. "I've seen it. He joined this

group with iNyanga and some other gods called the Circle of Truth. He's working to destroy the Board. That's why he's been trying so hard to find you. I think he's trying to prove he's changed."

Her expression was bitter. "I don't buy it. Why does he really need me?" She waved the piece of paper in the air. "What was he planning to get in exchange for this dagger?"

"I don't—how could you kn—"

"Magic, dear." She waved her hand in the air and the ink that had been washed off glowed. "Rama is nothing if not simple. Now, I'll ask again. What was he planning to get in exchange for this dagger?"

"I don't think I'm supposed to say," I said.

"You've told me everything else, and now you're clamming up?" Fire rose from her hand. "I don't think that's a good idea."

She was right.

"He wants his Brahmastra. He said there is a piece of it that can be molded to make a key. Apparently, he needs it to complete his plan."

She chuckled, shaking her head. "Then he's really trying to do it, is he? I thought we had more time."

"What is he trying to do?"

"You have been led astray, my dear," Kadlu said standing. "Rama has no interest in saving the universe."

"He doesn't?"

She raised her face to the ceiling and laughed again. "Don't get me wrong. He wants to dismantle the Board all right, but only so he can fill the power vacuum and rule the universe himself."

My brows knit. "How can he do that? He can't possibly be powerful enough to take on the whole of the Celestial Realm."

"Not by himself. He wants to open a door to the Dark Planet and harness the power of every being the gods fear in the ultimate hostile takeover, which is why he needs the key."

My jaw fell slack. I couldn't believe it. Rama was trying to save the universe...wasn't he? "Why should I believe you?"

She walked over to the window. "You don't have to. He'll reveal himself for the snake he is soon enough."

"I—I have to talk to Chelle." I grabbed the dragon fire ring on my nose and pulled it off, staring into it. All I saw was sparks of electricity, as the necklace on the other end of our connection jostled all over, showing glimpses of Chelle's face in pain. "Chelle!"

Kadlu stood up straight. "What is that?"

"It's my connection to my fiancé," I said. "She's in pain. She's hurt."

She snatched the ring from me. "This is a dragon fire gem, isn't it?"

I nodded dumbly.

"That is one of Rama's favorite ways to spy on his people." She crushed the gem. "We have to get out of here."

"I'm not going anywhere with you!"

But it was too late. A whistling sound seared the air and Kadlu leapt on top of me, knocking us both to the ground. Her office exploded into a million pieces and covered us with debris.

"You can stay if you want, but do you really want to trust the kind of person who would try to kill you just to get to me?"

Acid rain fell on my skin. I shook my head. "No, I don't."

Kadlu grabbed my hand. "Rose, if you betray me, not even a whole pantheon of gods can save you."

CHAPTER 48
RED

The alarms blared through the armory while yellow and red lights flashed, and long shadows and heavy boots marched through the aisles. There was no way for me to fight all of them, and until they disbursed it would be almost impossible to move through them. A moment of panic flooded through me, but then my training kicked in and my mind focused.

I locked the door to the cage and replaced the wooden tops onto the boxes inside, slipping inside the most spacious one, even though I could barely fit inside it and still close the lid properly. When I was safely inside, I closed my eyes and let my chest rise and fall more slowly with each breath.

"Check every cage!" a booming voice shouted. I winced as the jackboots clomped past me, sure I would be found out, but once they pulled on the cage to make sure it was locked, they continued on.

The base would be on high alert until a suspect was found, but I hoped that after a thorough check of the armory, they would assume that I escaped and move on to another part of the base. With every minute, I was losing my chance to kill Zeus. Every blare of the alarm was a stab in my heart telling me that another few seconds had been eaten away on my quest to save the universe.

"Gabrielle!" a strong voice whispered through the cage. "Are you in there?"

I poked my head out to see the apsara waving me forward, her feet naked and silent, bathed in the alternating yellow and red light. "What are you doing here? How did you get past the guards?"

"They were too distracted by the alarm. The moment they turned from me, I vanished from their sight. You know that's a special skill of mine."

I climbed out of the box and left the cage. "I'm so happy to see you."

"Be happy later," she said. "Follow me."

She grabbed my hand and pulled me toward the end of the row. As we reached it, two devas turned down the alley. My heart stopped for a second, but the apsara stood firm, and the devas didn't take notice of us. They continued on and disappeared from sight around the corner.

I let go of my breath. "That is quite a skill you have."

"Being unseen is of great value for a servant," she replied. "Now hurry. While I can stay hidden, I cannot go unseen if touched or heard."

We sped down the row and turned right before passing a group of angels patrolling the grounds. One of them seemed to see right into me, but then, her head jerked and she continued on her way. We finally came to the vent I was supposed to crawl through to Zeus's laboratory, but it was covered with laser beams.

"We can't go that way," I said.

The apsara looked both ways, and then nodded. She

grabbed my hand again and we snaked through the armory until we reached the front. The dead guard still laid by the door, looking out with cold, dead eyes. Blood oozed down through the metal grates beneath him. I stared back at him. In the Dream Realm it had been so easy to kill. Their souls were dusted from existence and evaporated into the ether. Here, it was different.

"Come on." The apsara pulled me through the door and away from the body.

When we exited, the apsara stopped cold and I slammed into her. "What are you—"

But I didn't need to finish. I followed her eyes to Athena, who stared back at us with fire in her eyes. "You!"

"What's happening? How can she see us? We didn't make a sound."

"I can't hide myself from gods," the apsara said, her tone defensive. "Go!"

She raised her arms and shot fireworks toward Athena. I didn't have time to argue. I turned and bolted, without even thanking her for helping me. I had barely turned the corner before I heard a thunderous boom and the walls quaked along with the floor, but I didn't stop.

Thankfully, the sanctuary wasn't filled with guards like the Crystal Keep, but diplomats. They didn't put up much of a fight as I flew past them towards Zeus's laboratory. I had lost the element of surprise but knew that this may very well be my only chance to kill the god. I wasn't going to stop until I took my shot.

"So predictable." A flash erupted when I reached the statues outside the Board's chambers. The statues of the gods pointed at me from every direction, and Athena materialized, holding her electric baton. "I'm glad I have a chance to fight you one on one, actually, to show you how pathetic you really are."

"You're not going to call for backup?"

Athena balled her fists. "The day I need any help to defeat a human is the day I lay down my baton."

I pulled the daggers from my belt and held them ready. "You won't be the first god I've killed, and you won't be the last I slaughter this day."

"At least you're confident. It's less fun when they've lost the will to fight."

She shot forward in a streak and swung at me. I barely ducked her attack and rolled away before she was on top of me again. I wasn't stupid. I knew that my odds of winning against a god were next to nothing, but I had to keep moving, avoiding her strikes until I could get a clean shot with the golden dagger. If Rama was right, then it was the only thing that could kill her.

Athena was strong and powerful, and she knew it, which made her attacks sloppy. She might have been the goddess of war, but her technique had deteriorated after years of terrorizing mere mortals.

She slammed her baton down, attempting an overhead smash, and I backflipped out of the way. Even with her bad form, she was quicker and stronger than any I had ever faced. Her attack crashed through the image of humanity cowering against the gods, and its destruction gave me an idea.

I rushed toward the closest statue, and she followed me, swinging wildly. When I reached the statue, just as I expected, she swung at me, and I ran up the edge of the statue and leapt backward, just as her baton cracked the base of the statue.

She screamed as the statue crashed down upon her. She

didn't even try to move out of the way. All she had time for was to hold up her hands to block it from smashing through her face. Its weight wouldn't kill her, but hopefully it would slow her down enough to give me a head start. I could take care of Zeus and escape before she came chasing after me.

CHAPTER 49
NIMUE

The door to Hastur's lair closed. I squeezed the maid's hand harder. "What is your name?"

"Is that important?" she asked.

"To me, it is. If I'm going to die today, I would like to know the name of the person I am dying for."

"Ferelda," she replied. "I do not want you to die for me."

"And I do not want you to die for my mistake," I said. "Perhaps providence will be on our side, and neither of us will die this day."

Neon lights flickered on the ground; blue, green, and orange speckled in the abyss. It reminded me of the Nightmare Realm, and its horrible, yet beautiful, native flora and fauna. The lights were suspended in midair throughout the room, like little droplets of illuminated water, and I avoided touching them on our way through.

"Ow," Ferelda said. I whipped my head around to see her arm splattered with orange goo. "It burns."

"Be careful," I replied. "Don't touch anything you see, no matter how alluring."

She nodded and followed me through the field of neon

droplets. They multiplied the further we went, until the only path forward involved crawling on our hands and knees, and then dropping to the ground and shuffling forward. Without warning, the droplets fell to the ground, splashing all over us. We both cried out as the neon sizzled on our bodies. It was over quickly, at least, and I turned back to Ferelda to find her shivering in agony.

"Are you okay?" I whimpered, trying to fight against the pain coursing through my own body.

She shook her head. "I will survive, for now."

With the neon dissipated, we were in black again. I pushed myself to my knees, and as I did a yellow glow lit the darkness, and then, after a second, two red eyes beamed into it.

"My dear Nimue. You have been busy, have you not?"

I stayed on my knees, supplicating to his power. "I know not what you mean, my lord."

"You nursed my beloved Delilah back to health, and met with my great nemesis, didn't you?"

It was impossible to argue. He wanted me to know that there was nothing that I could do which he didn't see. However, he didn't mention my meeting with Elvira, or any of the things I talked about with Cassandra, which meant that while he knew my actions, he could not discern my words. He wasn't omniscient.

"I did, my lord. And please know that I defended you against the Faceless Woman."

"Of course you did. That is the only thing saving you at this moment. If you had not, you would have been discarded to the dogs already." He looked over at Ferelda, who had crawled up next to me. "And now you come to me with a maid who slighted me?"

"I didn't, sire," Ferelda flubbed and stuttered. "I—"

She shook so fiercely that I thought she might pass out, and then her tears started coming again, big, sopping ones that covered her face and choked her.

"It's okay, Ferelda," I said, touching my hand to hers. "Let me do the talking, okay?"

She nodded, but when her mouth opened to speak, all that came out was a low wail.

"You wish to speak on this woman's behalf?" Hastur asked, flatly. "To beg for her life?"

I nodded. "It was my fault that she faltered in her duties. I was unaware that one could not interact with the help, and my outburst caused her to drop her laundry. In forty years, she never had another offense."

"But that makes it all the better. It is my greatest joy when they fail, and the longer they last without a mistake, the greater the fall when they finally do. Why should I deny myself the rapturous joy of pain?"

"She is a good worker, and thorough. You will not find another like her."

"I have found hundreds like her. I could have a thousand so close to her in appearance and temperament that you would not be able to tell them apart. They are servants, and they exist to serve my whims, whatever those may be." His eyes bore into me. "But you interest me, in your desire to speak for her. None of my other princesses would be so brazen. Tell me, will you take her punishment as your own?"

It took me a moment, but I answered meekly, "If you wish it, I will die on her behalf."

"And if I wish you to kill her, will you do it for me?" Hastur asked. "And remember before you answer, my princesses will do anything I say. If you choose the wrong answer, I will send you back to the dungeon."

The thought terrified me, but I would not let the woman die. "I will not kill her."

Hastur stalked towards me. "I have been too lenient on you. It is clear now I must break you like a horse." He squeezed my cheeks together. "I will bring so much pain onto you that you will beg to kill this nothing for me."

"And if I don't?" I asked, swallowing the fear bubbling up in the back of my throat.

"Then it is a win for me, because your pain is its own reward."

I stared deep into his eyes and spoke through gritted teeth. "Do your worst."

"Oh, my dear. I will. You can count on that."

CHAPTER 50
ARIEL

I couldn't help but laugh after Vivian revealed she intended to betray me, which took her off guard. "Why are you laughing? Stop it!"

"It's just—" I stopped laughing and my face hardened. "Did you really not think I would expect you to betray me?" I pulled a small round ball out of my pocket and held it up. "While you weren't looking, I took this from one of the shelves."

"What is it?"

"I don't know. It's just listed in the ledger as a defensive orb." A devious grin rose on my face. "Let's find out together."

I slammed the ball on the ground, and the explosion knocked me off of my feet. While I recovered, Vivian struggled to right herself. I didn't wait. I rushed around the nearest stack of weapons and pushed it with my shoulder, sending its contents crashing to the ground. She cursed me after me as I raced down the aisles.

An explosion rocked me, and a few seconds later Vivian leapt from the rubble and gave chase. I tucked the ledger tighter under my arm and pushed several aisles of objects down.

"You can't hide from me!" she screamed.

"I'm not trying to hide!" I shouted back, still scrambling. "I'm trying to escape."

The entrance at the end of the white aisles was easy to see, as it loomed above everything else. All I had to do was get out and trap Vivian inside, but she was gaining on me, and quickly.

"Enough!" Vivian leapt twenty feet forward. I reached onto the nearest shelf and pulled out a silver lance. It vibrated with power against my hands. I spun around and parried Vivian's trident knocking her off balance. She tumbled into the wreckage of the shelves.

"Why are you doing this?" I cried, dropping the ledger to free myself from her grasp. "The fate of the Dream Realm is on the line and you're trying to get this eye for some— why do you even want it?"

"Because it is power!" Vivian said, her eyes glinting. "It will allow me to leave this accursed place, like Agrona before me—and with the trident, and the eye. I will start a new life on Earth, in control of the land and the sea."

I scoffed. "Power? Really. How trite."

Vivian roared and lunged at me with the trident. I had little skill with the lance, but she was also inexperienced with her weapon, both of us too reliant on magic for our own good. As she continued her attacks, I grabbed anything I could find from the shelves and tossed them at her; silver orbs, pelts, tufts of moss, anything that wasn't bolted down. When none of it stopped her, I pulled down another shelf. It was an old classic, but it worked.

The vault door was right in front of me now, and with the lance in one hand and the eye in the other, I thought I had a good chance of locking her inside. My magic didn't work inside the vault, but once I was outside, I could push the door closed with my power.

Vivian jumped at me again and sliced my side with her weapon. In my last act of defense, I spun and threw the lance. It missed, but she was forced to dodge it, giving me the time I needed to leap out of the vault.

"*Dis clausi!*" I screamed. Two huge pink arms rose out of my body and pressed against the door. "Faster!"

"Tsk, tsk, tsk," I heard a smooth male voice. "That's no way to treat an emissary of mine, Ariel. I thought your mother taught you better than that."

I turned around and my face contorted in confusion. "Loki?"

"That's right, sister," Vivian said. "Now, I think you have something that belongs to me."

"Hand over the eye and we'll let you live," Loki said.

"Oh, don't make that promise, darling." Vivian kissed Loki square on the lips. "I am very much looking forward to killing her now that she has no use to me."

CHAPTER 51

RED

There was no time for subtlety, which was a shame, because I enjoyed the delicate art of subterfuge. However, Athena would be back in moments to defend Zeus. She was already shifting the statue from underneath. I needed to complete my mission quickly, assuming that Zeus was even still in his laboratory.

I reached the end of the hallway and held my golden dagger ready. Zeus was even more powerful than Athena, and I was facing him head on, the last thing I wanted to do. I needed to be quick and use the element of surprise to my advantage.

I took a deep breath and kicked in the door. I clocked him fiddling with the electrodes over Nox's uninhabited body, a dozen wires and tubes protruding from her limbs. I pushed off the balls of my feet and rushed towards him, raising the dagger over my head. For a moment, I thought I might actually succeed, but then he turned and smiled, lifting his hand to stop my motion.

"Oh, good," he said. "You've arrived."

He snapped his fingers and a side door opened. Two

guards emerged and threw Rama on the ground, beaten and bloodied, and Brahma next to him, locked in the same blue electric restraints used on me, but thicker and clearly more powerful.

"Rama!" I shouted.

"Don't worry about him," Zeus said, curling his fingers and forcing me closer to him. "He's done me a great service. The moment that the alarm bell rang, I knew whatever deception he and Brahma had been planning would come to fruition, and that it would involve you. I hope I did not make it too easy on you."

"Easy on me?" I said. "You planned this?"

It was impossible. Escaping from the armory was inconceivable, and it involved the apsara sacrificing herself to give me the time to—and what of Athena, who nearly killed me?

"Plan is such an—unwieldy word," he said. "I allowed it to happen, to expose the traitors in my midst." He held me in place with telekinesis as he walked around the lab table. "I realized what Nox wanted you for."

"What's that?"

"For years I have been looking for a way to consolidate the power of the gods." He placed a glass jar on a pedestal. "And you are the key to making it work."

"You're insane," I growled, struggling against the magic that held me in place. "Let me go."

He shook his head. "Why would I do that? You'll just try to kill me, and I can't have that, not when my friend tells me that the power contained inside you is greater than that of any other being in the universe." He smiled. "Imagine, concentrated magic so intense that a single drop of your blood could destroy a planet." He pulled my arms open with the power of his mind, and tubes rose from his console and bore into my skin. "If only you knew how to use it, what you could do with it is unfathomable."

His hand curled into a fist and then he flicked it open. Lightning coursed through me. I screamed out in pain and felt my life force draining. Across the room, the small jar filled with pink energy.

Still, though, I clung to my knife, unwilling to drop it. It was my one chance for redemption. Zeus was distracted, watching the jar fill up with energy, smiling to himself smugly. My eyes found Rama and Brahma. Their rebellion would be lost if he gained my power. Chelle and Rose would be found and destroyed.

"My dear, you are watching the dawn of a new age," Zeus said. "Aren't you proud of yourself?"

What had Zeus said about me being more powerful than the gods themselves? That if I only knew how to use my power, I could rise up...had my weak human brain held me back from realizing my true power?

The jar was half filled as Zeus turned back to it, his maniacal face lit with the pink energy that apparently bubbled from my very veins. I closed my eyes and concentrated on moving my arm, just an inch. I struggled against Zeus's will for a long moment, and then, like a rubber band, I snapped free. With the last ounce of my strength I flung the golden dagger at him.

Zeus barely had a chance to turn to see his folly before the blade plunged deep into his heart. He let out a startled gasp and then fell to the floor. I tumbled down with him, free.

Athena came into the room at the same moment. "What have you done?" she screamed, hurrying toward Zeus, who lay limp on the ground.

"She has done nothing wrong," Brahma replied. "Zeus

planned to overthrow the Board and consolidate power for himself. This woman saved us all. She is a hero."

"But—" Athena stared down at Zeus's dead body.

"You have a duty to the Board," Brahma added. "Not to Zeus. Do your duty and free us, so that we might put this unpleasantness behind us and decide how to move forward."

Athena's eyes ping-ponged back and forth between Zeus's dead body and Brahma, then she dropped her eyes and nodded.

I had just saved the universe, and yet, I felt like my job was far from over. In fact, it might have only just begun.

CHAPTER 52

NIMUE

Hastur stripped me bare and tied me to a rack. It was a primitive torture for a primitive beast, but it was effective. I didn't cry out the first time he lashed me, or the fifth, but by the tenth my eyes were tearing so badly that I couldn't keep from blubbering.

"Are you ready to do the deed, my dear?"

Ferelda stood next to the rack, crying as loudly as I wished I could, but I simply shook my head. This made him angrier, and his lashing became more ferocious. After five more lashes he pulled me off the rack and tied me upright, with my arms and legs extended as wide as they could go. Blood dripped down my back and I heard it splashing on the floor.

"I hate to see you like this, my love," Hastur purred.

"I know that is not true, my king." My voice was weak and cracked. "I only hope you will take your vengeance out on me, and leave your servant spared."

He didn't seem to like that answer much. He turned a large crank along the edge of the machine, causing my arms and legs to stretch ever so slightly from their joints. I'd gone numb from the lashes, but my arms and legs felt every bit of the fresh hell he put me through. I was able to stifle my screams until I felt my right arm pop from its socket.

"It does not have to be this way," he said. "You could be a great princess to me."

"I have been a queen," I growled. "I could never go backwards."

He moved closer and whispered into my ear, "And if I made you my queen, would you take care of this matter for me?"

"Are your words true, king?" I asked. "Would you make me a queen, above all others?"

With the crown of a queen, I could gather the power to destroy Hastur outright, with or without the princess's support.

"The others are little more than children," he continued, circling me now, "but you are something exceptional. You would make an exquisite queen, with dominion above all others in Carcosa…in the whole world, besides me. Is that what you want?"

I very much wanted power, all of it, every single bit of it, and to never be tortured or debased again. "You would not be able to have me, not until our wedding day, my king, if I were to agree, and I would need dominion over the housing staff, so that they could not be taken by you, either."

He exhaled loudly. "The fact that you still deny me—it is intoxicating. If that is your wish, my dear, I can make it happen."

"And the princesses," I said. "They will not be harmed. I will take their punishment, but please remember that I must look queenly for my coronation."

"None other has ever been my equal in this place, but you…I smell old power on you, and the approval of the old gods flows through you. This would be the marriage of such power as this world has never seen." He ran his fingers along my jaw. "You must submit to me whenever I request it, no matter how petty. Should you refuse, even once, our engagement is off."

"As long as you do not ask me to hurt the staff or the other princesses, I will submit to your every whim, master." I cleared my throat. "After the wedding, of course. Until then, none are to be harmed inside these walls."

"Very well." He cocked his head. "With one exception."

"What is it, my king?"

He spun to Ferelda. "You must kill this servant, right now, to prove your loyalty."

I knew the end game now. I saw it so clearly. I needed to move closer to the beast, in order to end him forever. What was one sacrifice, compared to the whole of the world? His sadistic pleasure would be to push me to my limits and force me to do things that I refused to do, but that was what intrigued him, too. He would see it as a win, but it would be his first fatal flaw, the one that would lead to his eventual defeat.

"I have done worse for less," I said.

"Then you agree?" He said, his voice almost rapturous.

I dropped my head. "I do."

"No," Ferelda screamed. "You promised!"

She fell to her knees as Hastur screamed out in laughter and let my good arm free. I lifted it up to Ferelda's face and connected with her eyes. "I'm sorry."

I closed my eyes and cast fire from my hands, burning her alive. My heart broke open with her shrieks, but then it sewed shut again, even tighter than it had been before, and I remembered what it meant to be a queen. Sacrifice and duty above all, in the pursuit of your ultimate goal, no matter who it hurt.

The world would be better without Hastur, but Ferelda would not see it.

CHAPTER 53

ROSE

I followed Kadlu down the stairs of the animal shelter and into a corridor under the building. "These tunnels lead through the city. Nobody uses the streets anymore. It was how I knew immediately you must be from somewhere else."

"Of course," I said. "It would have been nice if Rama told me that."

"Either he didn't know, or he wanted you to stick out from the crowd, to make it easier for me to find you. Now come, this way."

It made sense how confused everyone was that I had come to the front door when there were corridors that connected most of the major arteries together. They were thin, and not well trafficked, but that was because most of the people in the city were dead, and only the most bitter and scrappy had survived.

"It's really a testament to the human condition," Kadlu said. "The gods tried their best to wipe this place off the map and make it uninhabitable, but you humans just won't die, will you?"

I shrugged. "I guess not. We're a bit like cockroaches in that way."

Kadlu laughed. "Most of my brethren would tell you that is an insult to cockroaches. You are as hated to them as cockroaches are to you, and equally as useless."

The tunnel broke into an opening filled with dozens of tents, each one selling something or another, from roasted insects to disgusting soups. Kadlu turned her nose up on them, but not at the people serving them.

"Why are you here?" I asked. "It's not a dignified place for a god."

She turned and stuck her hand over my mouth, her eyes darting for a moment between the people populating the cavern. "Don't you dare say that here. These people will riot at the mere implication—" She pulled her hand away. "Just keep up, and don't say anything else stupid."

I stayed quiet, following Kadlu through the crowd and to a clearing on the other side where a path led to a small shack. Once we were inside, she locked the storm door before sitting across from me.

"I'm going to tell you something that will get you killed if anybody finds out you know. This is your one chance to walk away."

"I'm not going anywhere."

"No, I suppose you wouldn't. I see the determination in your eyes. It is a piteous combination of foolishness and bravery." Her eyes narrowed. "The god you know is not Rama. It looks like him, and moves like him, but it is not the man I loved."

"You loved Rama?" I asked.

"Once, a long time ago, before he changed into something else. Something unnatural."

"How do you know?"

"Have you ever loved somebody?"

I thought of the dragon fire ring that laid crushed on the ground of the animal shelter and looked down at the invisible ring on my hand. "I love somebody."

"Then you know how to tell if they are not themselves. It is—they are just different, from the big things, like how they kiss, to the small ones, like how they tie their shoes. We worked together, for a long time, to bring down the Board, but one day, something changed in him. While the things he said were the same as before, the actions he took became more...circuitous."

"Maybe he just fell out of love with you, or was cheating on you?"

Kadlu laughed. "We cheated on each other all the time, and still loved each other deeply. No, this was something else." She turned from me and scavenged through a pile of trash, eventually pulling out a bag. "Do you see this?"

I took the bag and looked at it. "It looks like sand to me."

"It is an ancient bug, older than any of us even, that existed seemingly before this universe was created. I found it when I was retracing Rama's steps, trying to find out what was wrong with him. It invaded my poor Rama's brain and took it over."

"Like a spore?"

She nodded. "I don't know its plan, but I know it is desperate to open the door to the Dark Planet, which is why I have dedicated my life to stealing every piece of metal which could be forged to make the key."

"Like the Brahmastra?"

She walked over to a shelf and pulled a large spear. It was magnificent. She bent down and showed me its tip. "This metal, it can kill a god, and it is the only material that can open the door to the Dark Planet. It is the rarest substance in the universe."

"It looks like gold," I said, staring at it.

"Close in appearance maybe, but it is infinitely stronger. We used to use it for our armor to protect ourselves from the worst attacks."

"Like the armor in the Underworld? I always wondered why their gold didn't melt."

Kadlu shook her head. "Persephone's soldiers wear a poor imitation of the real thing." Her eyes narrowed again. "Have you ever seen anything like this weapon?"

My eyes went wide. "Yes, the golden dagger. The one I was showing you. My friend Gabrielle, it was her weapon. She killed Epiales with it."

"And where is it now?" she asked.

"It was taken by the Board when they captured her."

"Then we don't have much time," she said. "If we don't stop him from forging the blade into a key, then the universe is in great danger. Will you help me?"

I nodded. "If what you tell me is the truth, then my friends are in danger."

"Everyone is in danger."

CHAPTER 54

ARIEL

"Loki!" I shouted, wheeling on Vivian. "You're working with Loki?"

She laughed. "Don't be so surprised, kitten. We had a common grievance."

"And what's that?"

"You," Loki hissed. "Did you really think you could take one of my handmaidens, swear fealty to that worm, Hypnos, and I would just let that slight stand?"

I flung my arms in the air. "That was hundreds of years ago!"

"Yes, and I thought I handled it back then, but you survived, didn't you? And then Ursula took you in and Nox took pity on your poor little soul."

"Wait." My face pinched as I calculated his words. "You're responsible for my mother's death."

"She's not your mother!" Vivian cried out. "You will literally imprint on anything, won't you? She was just a kind woman, a stupid woman, just like Ursula."

"Ursula helped raise you!"

"Raised! I was an adult already when I came here. She

did nothing but hold me down." Vivian snatched the box from my hands. "And now, with the trident and the eye, we will escape this place and take our rightful places as rulers of Earth."

"That's thinking too small, my love," Loki said, with another kiss. "First Earth, then the universe."

"I don't think so," a low voice growled. I gasped and smiled when Hypnos emerged from a flash of light. "I was wondering when you should show yourself, Loki."

Loki dropped his arms from around Vivian and stammered. "Hypnos? What are you doing here?"

"Watching and waiting for you to emerge." He clapped his hands together and thick, golden chains wrapped around Loki's wrists. "All of my charges have been dealt with, but you. I believe I have a nice cell for you in my private dungeon."

"No, please, Hypnos! You—you don't understand."

"I heard everything, Loki. Now stop groveling like a child."

"Fine." Loki snatched for the box. Vivian held onto it as best she could, but Loki was a god, and he overpowered her in a matter of seconds. "I'll take my leave then. Until next time, Hypnos."

"I don't thi—" Hypnos started, but before he could raise his hand to subdue Loki, the trickster god snapped his fingers and disappeared in a puff of smoke and crackle of lightning.

"That is not ideal, but I will deal with him later." Hypnos growled in disgust before he turned his sights on Vivian. "You will tell me all you know about Loki's plans if you wish to remain in my realm un—what's the word you use for it?—dusted, I believe. Yes, undusted."

Vivian's demeanor changed completely with the emergence of Hypnos. Her head slung low, and her whole body trembled. The confidence and bravado she showed just moments before washed away, replaced with the air of a sniffling dog standing in their own pee, hoping not to be punished by their owner. "Your majesty, it would be my honor."

"Yes, it would." He snatched the trident from her and snapped his fingers, vanishing her as well. "Ursula has been looking for this. And as for you—" He looked at me and I thought I was in some trouble until he smiled. "You have done very well, Ariel. I'm so sorry to have you go through these hoops, but there was no other way to suss out Loki's plans. I hope you're not too cross with me."

I shook my head. "No, sir. I am just happy you trusted me to carry out your wishes."

"You don't have to lie to me. I'm not my mother. I know it sucked, and I want you to know I appreciated it."

I dropped my head. "Thank you, sir."

Hypnos sucked his teeth. "I'm afraid I have more to ask of you though, if you will help me once again."

"Anything, my liege."

He stepped forward. "This eye is incredibly powerful, and the Fates were right to believe that the future of the Dream Realm rests on finding them both. Will you help me find the right eye of Rapunzel?"

"If you wish it, then I will help you." I had no desire to anger the god of Dreams, and it seemed our goals were aligned. "Where must I go?

"I'm afraid it's in the one place even I fear to tread."

"Where is that?" I asked, suddenly frightened.

"The Nightmare Realm."

EPILOGUE
NIMUE

When he was done with me, Hastur handed me a white gown and I stumbled outside. I waited until the door slammed for the tears to start. I refused to let him know how horrible it had been inside that room.

"You okay?"

I looked up to see Elvira, Delilah, and Cassandra leaning against the wall across from me. Lydia and Bethel were walking towards me. I glanced between each of them, and I began to sob. They gathered around me, wrapping me in their arms. It was awkward, and I doubted any of them had a kind word to say to each other. However, in that moment, we were a very screwed up type of sisterhood.

"It's okay, Nimue," Cassandra said.

I met her eyes. "Call me queen."

She blinked. "Q-queen?"

I nodded. "I have agreed to take all your punishments, any time he desires, for as long as he desires, and in return, he will not lay a hand on any of you again."

Elvira shook her head. "You can't—you'll die."

"I have dealt with worse," I shot back, but my voice wavered.

Delilah shook her head. "You don't understand. He has taken many queens in his time, and none have lasted for more than two weeks after their coronation."

"For all the viciousness he heaps onto us," Cassandra added. "His ire is taken out tenfold on his queen."

I dropped my head. "Then, I guess we should find a way to kill him before we marry, and my payment to him comes due."

The hallway went silent after that, as the princesses looked at each other, skeptically but knowingly, and then nodded their heads, slowly at first, and then with more fervor.

The King in Yellow must die. I knew that, and as they all wrapped themselves around me, I was sure they knew it too. Through all of the pain, a jolt of happiness shot through me, and I smiled.

AUTHOR'S NOTE

This book was intense, especially writing Nimue's part. She still hasn't killed Hastur, and I thought she'd do that by the end of the last book. In fact, we're behind schedule now because she decided to take some detours. The Dark Planet is supposed to be opened, and she's supposed to be on the search for the rest of Rapunzel's face.

It's a wonderful part about writing books, that you can surprise yourself so often.

The fact that Rama and the others were supposed to have the key already, and Nimue was supposed to be free (and Rapunzel's pawn) meant I had to change the whole arc of this book when that changed. Nimue was supposed to spend the rest of this series going through each realm we had already visited before and wreaking havoc. Instead, she has had havoc brought upon her.

Nimue is a hard character to write. I want so badly to sympathize with her—with every character I write—but she is at best chaotic neutral, and more likely chaotic evil, which means anything that she goes up against must be more evil than she is in order for me to side with her.

It might be weird, but I absolutely believed in her quest in the first arc, as evil as she was. All she wanted was to get back to Earth and live a normal life. With that goal accomplished, I thought she would be happy, but when I went to plan the next book in the series, I realized being a nothing would be miserable for her.

The last arc was all about bringing Nimue back to glory as a queen, and then laying her low. She did some wicked stuff in the last arc, and in order to keep her sympathetic, I needed to make a character even more heartless and evil as she was to fight against, which ended up being Hastur, the King in Yellow. I wanted to explore their relationship. In this book, you didn't get a lot of it. It was mostly Nimue's machinations and positioning herself to take him down. I'm excited for their battle of wits in the next book, and to find out whether he lives or dies, because I have no idea right now. I keep thinking I know he's going to die, but Red was supposed to die in the sixth book, and yet, she's still alive and kicking.

One thing I was trying to avoid in this arc was separating Chelle and Rose unnecessarily. They had just gotten together, yet again, and I wanted them to keep in contact, which was why they got the dragon fire jewelry. I really wanted to have a moment where they spoke to each other, but the book had different ideas, and at the end of this book you are unsure if Chelle is even alive, and Rose has been thrust into trusting yet another god.

Speaking of, that turn with Rama was pretty crazy, right? Yeah, that wasn't in the original outline, either. Rama was supposed to be a good guy throughout, but then as I was writing I realized that no gods were really all good or all bad in the end. Kadlu was supposed to be a minor character who only appeared in a couple of scenes, but the moment I started writing her, I knew she had to be more involved, and so the plot became even more detailed.

The original plan for this series was to have sixteen books across four different arcs. I finally pulled the trigger on it and bought the new covers, which meant I needed to seed some things in these pages that wouldn't pay off for a couple more novels. That was the reason that Rama's revelation had to happen...but, of course, with this series, there's always the question of who the good guy is when the dust settles.

This arc really has certainly gotten away from my original vision, as you can probably tell. The overall beats are still there, and through the hazy fog I can still see the end game that I envisioned, but Rapunzel was supposed to be a much bigger part of the first couple of books, Hastur and the princesses were supposed to be less involved, and the Celestial Realm was supposed to—well, I don't want to give too much away.

Speaking of the princesses, though. They are the real reason Hastur has survived this long. They are my favorite part of this arc, and if I had killed Hastur already, I wouldn't have gotten to spend as much time with them. Now, I get a whole additional book, maybe more, to play with them, and get to know them better. Dark, brooding, beautifully haunted Goth princesses are 100 percent my jam, and I am here for it.

Who knows? Maybe one will even become a main character in the next book, *The Golden Locket*. You'll just have to read it and find out. Despite, or maybe because of, the chaotic nature of writing this arc, I'm really enjoying where it's going, and how I've been able to delve deep into both

The Celestial Realm and The Dark Planet. I hope you're enjoying it as much as I'm enjoying writing it. We're two books away from the conclusion of this arc, finding out Nox's plan, and discovering the fate of both realms.

THE GOLDEN LOCKET
PREVIEW
BOOK 11 OF THE OBSIDIAN SPINDLE SAGA

By:
Russell Nohelty

Edited by:
Leah Lederman

Proofread by:
Katrina Roets

Cover by:
JV Arts

Formatting by:
Turbo Kitten Industries

Nimue

I chose to marry Hastur. It was a rash decision, made in the heat of the moment, but I had agreed to it all the same, and couldn't back out now without consigning myself immediate torture and likely death. Now, all I could do was live with the consequences of my decision.

"Are you sure this is wise?" Cassandra asked after Hastur sent me away and I fell into her arms on the way back to my room. "Those who have resigned themselves to that fate have never lived to see their wedding night."

"It was absolutely not wise, but it was the only choice I had to make."

She brought me back to my room and tried to heal me, but the wounds were magically imbued to prevent such things. I had learned as much when I nursed Delilah back to health after her beating at his fingers during my first days in the castle. The pain was written all over her face then, but she refused to show it, and I did my best to mimic her stoic power now. Unfortunately, I had never been good with physical pain, and Beatrice's body was not accustomed to it, either, which made it all the harder to keep from writing how deeply I suffered all over my face.

"I made him promise not to touch me until the wedding, in lust or in anger," I replied, willing myself from wincing with every bit of strength left inside of me. "And he swore not to touch any other for as long as I obeyed him. Weddings take time to plan, so that should buy me a few months at least."

Cassandra placed her hand on the lacerations on my muscles. She still wore my skin, and the touch of it dug as deeply as Hastur's lashes on my back. I had hated her for it once. However, in my short time in the castle I grew to understand her plight better and sympathized with her.

There was no love lost between any of the princesses that served at the King in Yellow's behest. It was a constant struggle not to fall into his crosshairs, and that more than anything caused them to be catty and cold to each other. They would turn on each other in an instant to avoid his wrath, and that drove Cassandra to act. It was a wicked deed, but the longer I knew Hastur, the more I understood why she did it, and how she had little choice in the matter.

I hoped that my sacrifice at the dark lord's hand would bind them together against a common enemy. Now, they did not have to worry about the misery he brought upon them. I would take all their punishment, for as long as I was able, and shield them from pain until my dying breath.

"He has never kept his word when it did not further his ends. He will find a way to manipulate your words against you."

My skin fell from her face, loose and unhealthy. She looked more a monster now than she did without skin, truth be told, but she was also one of the few women in the universe who understood my plight, which made me trust her implicitly even given her past transgressions.

"I have no doubt of that, Cassandra, but I have dealt with powerful men who wished me ill all my life. I have supreme confidence that I can bend the king to my will, and not the other way around."

The muscles of her mouth twitched, but her skin did not move with them. "I appreciate your confidence, Nimue, but you have never seen one as cruel and manipulative as the King in Yellow. He is every bit the equal of any other in malice and cruelty. To think otherwise is folly."

I pushed myself to stand despite the pain. "Can you please wrap me in the gauze Bethel left on the table so that I do not bleed through my dress?"

"Of course," Cassandra replied, rising and taking the wrap from the table. "What do you plan to do?"

I raised my hands above my head. "Bring down a god, of course, before he can terrorize any others, or kill me."

Cassandra wrapped the gauze around my chest, pulling it taut so that it didn't slip. Every time she passed my wounds, it sent a shiver of pain through my body.

"I'm sorry," she said. "The pain will be over soon."

"You are wrong," I replied. "I will have to withstand an untold amount before the end. That much I know for sure. I only hope I can survive long enough to find the king's weakness and take him down."

She ripped the gauze with her teeth and pressed it tightly down against my side. "If there is a weakness in the king, I do not know it, and no others have mentioned a whisper of it in my presence."

I lowered my arms and went to my closet. "You have never spoken with all your sisters at once before, have you?"

She shook her head. "No. Sometimes I dined with Elvira, and I had tea with Delilah on occasion, but the others walled themselves off from me, preferring solitude, or each other's company."

I slid a slip over my shoulders, the soft cloth of it burning my back with even the slightest touch. "And that has worked to Has—" I remembered then that there was an enchantment in using his name, which called him forth and let him sneak in on any conversation. "—the king's advantage. Today, we eliminate that advantage."

"How?" Cassandra asked.

"Together, the six of us are more powerful than any one alone. I believe between us, we can find a weakness in him, and exploit it." I faced her. "I still do not completely trust you, but in this place, you are the only that I can give this task. Call the princesses together. Tell them it is of utmost importance that I see them immediately."

"And if they will not come?"

In the moments after my lashing, the six of us came together in a way I didn't think possible, as a unit, and agreed to work together in an effort to kill Hastur and take his head as our trophy. However, it was a fractious partnership, and Cassandra was right to question it. I did not have that luxury. If I didn't believe fully in our alliance, then I was condemning myself to death.

"They will come. They must. Their future queen demands it."

A black statue in the corner of the room let out a loud shriek, and in its wake, my betrothed spoke in a booming voice. "Nimue, I have need of you."

The statue fell silent. Cassandra shook with fear, and her eyes, hidden partially behind the flaps of my forehead, were wide with panic.

"It's okay, my friend. I have used what power I have to safeguard this room from prying ears." I said in a soft voice. "Call the princesses and have them meet together once I am done with him."

"And if you do not survive this encounter?"

I smirked at her. "Better men have tried and failed, but if the worst happens, then it falls on you to carry the torch, and make me a martyr to the cause."

"I don't know if I can do that."

I placed my hand on her loose face and cradled my own cheek along with hers when I did so. "I believe in you."

"Why?" She said, softly, turning into my hand. "I have done nothing to prove that kind of faith."

"Because I must, Cassandra. Because we all must. Killing the King in Yellow is everything for every one of us. It is all that matters."

ARIEL

After defeating Loki, Hypnos led us back to his palace, where he secured both the god of mischief and my sister deep in the bowels of the Emerald City. When we finally emerged from the darkness back into the glimmering emerald gleam of the castle, he turned to me with a glint in his pink eyes.

"Thank you for your service to the Dream Realm," he said with a dour tone to his voice. "I hate to ask more of you, but there are few I trust among gods or men anymore."

"Why is that?" I asked.

"The reasons are complicated but—I have never been a social butterfly, mind you, but in the past years, a sickness has spread among my people. One that has turned even the righteous selfish and twisted the weak-willed into the worst kind of monster." He sighed. "As for humanity, they were created in our image, with all the ego and self-centeredness, but without an eternity to temper their tempers, they look only to the nearest moment, and never to the long-term. They cannot be trusted, save for ones like you, who do the right thing for its own sake."

I furrowed my eyebrows. "I do not know about all that, but I have lived in the dark for too long not to move to the light now."

For almost three hundred years, I lived in the underwater castle of Ursula, queen of the sea, blind to the machinations of the surface world, unaware of the light that existed just out of my reach. Now that I had felt the light on my face, I had no interest in fumbling around in the darkness ever again.

"Those are prescient words, and they give me pause, as what you must do now will take you into a darkness like you have never experienced."

My eyes narrowed. "You're talking about the Nightmare Realm."

It was not a question, but a statement of fact. Hypnos told me that the right eye of Rapunzel laid there when he saved me from my duplicitous sister, and that it was incumbent on me to find it.

"I am," he replied. "Even though my brother is dead, I have been barred from entering it, and even if I did, none would trust me enough to give direction to my quest. Unlike this place, that I control with every inch of my being, I am as ineffective in Sprig as a child cast adrift in a vast ocean."

"I understand," I replied. "If you have need of Rapunzel's eye to save the Dream Realm, then I will do my duty and deliver it to you, my lord."

"I hoped you would say as much." He held out his palm to me. "Then take my hand."

I placed my hand into his and together we vanished into the abyss. We materialized again on the top of a giant mountain, high above the plains of Oz. A range of snow-topped mountains expanded into the horizon, and a chilly bitterness whipped against my cheek.

"This is the Mountain Realm, isn't it?" I asked, breathlessly. I had spent so much time below the sea that the idea of staring down at the whole of the world was completely foreign to me. The whole range of mountains speckled the sky, but we stood above them all.

"Yes," Hypnos replied. "And this is what remains of Agrona's castle."

A horrible mouth, carved into the mountain, spewed rock that clogged any from entering, though I had no idea why any would want to do so. My eyes craned up to see the whole of the mountain top had collapsed on the terrible cavern.

Hypnos clapped his hands together and placed them on the edges of the mouth door. I watched as time stood still, and then seemed to fold back in on itself. Whatever damage befell the great keep disappeared as rocks reformed around it, creating a hallway lined with paintings, and a spongy tongue plumped up to carry us onward. When he was done, the collapsed mountain looked as pristine as if it had not collapsed inside itself. The snowy mountain top glistened like its brethren around it, shining like a beacon above them all.

Hypnos beckoned me forward. My bare feet touchy the spongy tongue and the feel of the rough, course, undulating ground sent a shudder up my spine. However, I stayed behind him, clinging closer than seemed comfortable, hoping for protection from anything that dared to attack in the darkness.

The hallway broke into a pristine throne room, but Hypnos did not focus on any of its many treasures. Instead, his eyes found a tall, faceless wall that rose thirty feet or more into the air.

"Yes, I can feel its power here," Hypnos said as he moved closer to the wall.

"What power?" I asked.

He turned to me. "Maybe Agrona didn't even know it when she chose this as her castle, but the veil between Urgu and the Nightmare Realm is thinner here than anywhere else in the Dream Realm. No wonder she worked so hard to keep me from this place."

He returned to examining the wall, running his fingers along the rough surface of it. It took him several minutes to finish his inspection before he placed his palm on a rock in the middle of the wall.

"This is how I will enter the Nightmare Realm?"

He nodded. "I can almost push my fingers through to the other side myself, but it is just out of my grasp. Powerful as I am in this place, my mother set limits on what my brother and I could do." He held up the eye. "However, with this, I believe I can make a path to the other side."

My heart leapt into my chest. I had only heard stories of the monsters that came through from the Nightmare Realm, and of the great battles waged to save the Dream Realm from complete destruction. Could I hope to survive the monstrosities I would face on the other side of the portal?

"Are you sure this is a good idea?" I asked. "The last time this portal was opened, Urgu was infested with horrible monsters."

"I was not here, then," Hypnos said. "Please trust that I know what I'm doing, both in opening this portal, and choosing you to venture into the other side as my champion."

I took a deep breath. "I will...I do...trust you I mean."

"Then let us begin."

He closed his eyes and muttered under his breath for a long time. As he did the air whipped through the room, and then, with a thunderous boom, an enormous red portal swirled in front of me, half the size of the wall itself.

"I will keep it open as long as I can," he replied. "But make haste. My power is great, but it is not infinite."

"How will I find the eye?" I asked, the booming sound of the vacuous void forcing me to scream to be heard even as I walked closer.

"The eye craves power. Follow where it leads, and you will find the eye."

I wished that the gods would speak plainly, without riddles and double-speak, but that was not their way. This was as good as I would get from a god. It wasn't even clear he knew what he was doing when it came to the eye, but what was clear as I stepped through the portal was from this point I was on my own.

"Do you see this here?" Kadlu said, holding up a baggy of blue crystals. We had not poked our head above ground in three days, nervous that Rama and whatever cabal he hired to kill Kadlu would be on the hunt if we did so. For the most part, we stayed in the shack that acted as the goddess's safehouse from the acid rain that pounded outside and whoever wanted her dead.

Rama didn't want me dead along with Kadlu, even if he had a funny way of showing it. If he did, I never would have agreed to go back to the Celestial Realm to save his life from whatever organism was eating his brain.

"It looks like rock salt," I replied.

She looked over at the bag. "It does at that, but don't put it on your dinner. It will literally kill you if you're not infected with the Spore."

This morning Kadlu left the safehouse early in a frenzy after receiving a phone call on a line that I thought dead. The phone attached to it had been mostly eaten by the acid water that slid under the foundation and leaked into the room most of the day, leaving only the half-eaten receiver and a speaker box hanging loosely.

She didn't say a word when the phone call came in. She simply leapt up and dashed through the door without saying goodbye. We weren't the best of friends, but over the days of isolation we had shared stories about each other's lives. Not much at first, being wary of each other for many reasons. Her because there had been an attempt of her life moments after I sauntered into her office, and me because of all the terrible things Rama said about her.

But soon the truth came into focus, at least from Kadlu's perspective. If she was to be believed, then Rama was the evil one. Somehow, a plague, or a spore, had infected her love and turned him against her, warping his brain and twisting it to a path of conquest and destruction. I found it a hard pill to swallow, especially because the cause Rama backed when I first met him was to bring down the Board and institute democratic elections in the Celestial Realm for the first time in eons.

"Then don't give it to me, you loon," I replied when she tried to hand it to me.

Of course, if he was to be trusted, then why did he try to kill me? I had gone over it a hundred times since the explosion in Kadlu's office, and nothing else made sense. Rama and I were the only two people who knew my plan, save for Chelle, and she would never turn on me.

Gods, I missed her.

"We don't have much choice in the matter. Rama trusts few, and you have won his graces."

I allowed her to place the plastic bag in my hand. "If he trusts me, then why did he try to kill me?"

"It wasn't personal," Kadlu replied, her face soft and

glowing. "He would do anything to kill me and gain what I have taken from him. Which reminds me—"

She pulled the brahmastra from the far end of the shack. It glistened and glowed as she held it. The lance-like weapon had been used by Rama to slay the demon king Ravana and earn his place as a god.

"It's incredible that he would kill you for something so trivial as a weapon."

"Not the whole weapon." She pointed to the gold inlaid in the blade. "Just this part of it, that he can use to forge a new key to the Dark Planet and bring forth untold evil onto the world."

"Are you sure we should be giving it back to him, then?" I asked, hesitant.

She bit her lip. "I am not sure about much, but without it, you will be questioned. If you bring this back with you, his excitement will overpower his common sense."

I held up the plastic bag. "And that is when I use this?"

She nodded. "If I'm right, then this will kill the disease controlling his brain, and give him clarity for the first time in an age."

"What is it?" I stared closely at it.

She sighed. "It's magic, old, dark, deep magic; the type which shouldn't be called without good reason, because it could disrupt the foundation of our whole universe."

I smiled at the bag. "Oh great. That's all I need, to cause the destruction of the cosmos."

"Without it, whatever has infected Rama's brain will take root even deeper, and with every passing moment, its horrible vision grows from an impossibility to an improbability, and eventually manifests into an inevitability. We must disrupt that paradigm before there is no turning back."

"Okay," I replied. "You've made your point. Please, no more speeches."

She reached over and opened the bag. I jittered as she pulled a single crystal out using just her thoughts and left it hovering between us. "This is enough to destroy the spores."

I looked down at what was left. "And what about the rest of this?"

"He will not be the only one turned, and with any luck his memory will lead us to the others." She pointed to the bag. "The rest is for them."

"Oh great," I replied. "An army of infected gods. That's just peachy."

"Listen carefully." She concentrated on the crystal. "*Sahaq.*" She crystal jittered in the air and crumbled into fine dust. "*Rih.*"

She flicked her fingers and the dust plumed across the room. I scooted back on my butt until I slammed against the wall. The ground was still wet with acid rain, and the burning under my hand made me scream out in pain. The sand neared my mouth, but just as it did, the sand stopped in midair, and then retreated into Kadlu's hands.

"That is all it takes," she said. She muttered another incantation and the sand reformed into a crystal, which she placed back into the bag. "Remember those words."

I zipped the bag back. "I will."

"Then I have nothing else to show you." She handed the brahmastra to me. "May the gods carry you on your journey."

"And not stop me before I can fulfill it."

She smiled. "Well spotted. Probably not the best idea to invoke the gods right now."

"Not when they are trying to kill us," I replied.

"Not all of us." She smiled. I didn't know whether she meant not all gods were trying to kill us, or that the gods weren't trying to kill all of us, but before I could ask, she rose to her feet and opened the hatch to the tunnels underneath the city. "We must make haste. There is no time to wait. Every second we delay brings Rama's doom closer to fruition."

ALSO BY RUSSELL NOHELTY

The Obsidian Spindle Saga

The Godsverse Chronicles

Ichabod Jones: Monster Hunter

Cthulhu is Hard to Spell

My Father Didn't Kill Himself

Sorry for Existing

Gumshoes: The Case of Madison's Father

The Invasion Saga

The Vessel

Worst Thing in the Universe

The Void Calls Us Home

The Marked Ones

The Little Bird and the Little Worm

Gherkin Boy

Find a complete list at

https://www.russellnohelty.com/books/

About the Author

Russell Nohelty is a USA Today bestselling author, publisher, and speaker. He is the author of dozens of novels and graphic novels including The Godsverse Chronicles, The Obsidian Spindle Saga, and Ichabad Jones: Monster Hunter. He has a very entertaining newsletter, which you can join at www.russellnohelty.com. He lives in Los Angeles with his wife and dogs.

Get one of my favorite books for free at:
    www.russellnohelty.com/mail
    Substack:
    https://authorstack.substack.com
    Bookbub:
    https://www.bookbub.com/profile/russell-nohelty